THE LAST OF THE JEDI

RETURN OF THE DARK SIDE

STAR WARS

LAST OF THE JEDI

STAR WARS

THE LAST OF THE JEDI

RETURN OF THE DARK SIDE

Jude Watson

SCHOLASTIC INC.

New York Toronto London Auckland Sydney
Mexico City New Delhi Hong Kong Buenos Aires

www.starwars.com
www.scholastic.com

ISBN-13: 978-0-439-68139-1
ISBN-10: 0-439-68139-1

12 11 10 9 8 7 6 5   8 9 10 11 12/0

Printed in the U.S.A.
First printing, December 2006

RETURN OF THE DARK SIDE

CHAPTER ONE

Almost there.

Ferus Olin ran through the last check on Platform-7, the BRT droid computer that ran the capital city of Sath. It had taken over two days of constant monitoring, but most systems were back to full function. And, most important to Ferus, any information that could lead to the discovery of the identities of the Samarian resistance was gone.

Now what?

He wasn't sure what he was doing here on Samaria. It had been a spur-of-the-moment decision; he'd sent off his friends to safety, but he had remained. He felt an obligation to help the Samarians straighten out their immediate problems, and make sure that the computer sabotage hadn't endangered any members of the resistance.

But this wasn't his battle. He had set his own mission — to find every Jedi who had managed to escape Imperial Order 66, who had survived the Empire's slaughter. He'd set up a secret base for them on an unmapped asteroid. But it seemed as though every time he was about to focus on his mission, he was knocked off course.

Obi-Wan would never let this happen to him. Why does it keep happening to me?

It was true that since he'd started, he'd found two Jedi. He'd been through high-speed chases, a trip to the ruined Jedi Temple, and a stay in an Imperial prison. He'd been pursued by a bounty hunter and an Inquisitor. He'd been to the Outer Rim and under the crust of Coruscant. He was starting to get the feeling that surviving Jedi were few and far between.

There has to be a better way to do this.

The Emperor had offered him amnesty in exchange for fixing the computer-sabotage problem in Sath, adding almost as an afterthought that Ferus's partner and best friend might die if Ferus didn't do it. Ferus had taken the job.

And so, Ferus Olin, double agent, was born.

He wore the label uneasily. He didn't like working for the Empire, even though he was trying to undermine it at the same time. He didn't like being this close to the dark side.

Ferus felt a sudden lurch in his stomach, a feeling

close to nausea. Darth Vader was near. One of the things he'd learned staying here in Imperial head-quarters was that the Sith could be hard on the digestion.

The door slid open in the darkened room. Darth Vader stood in the doorway. He never entered a room unless he had to. He was a busy . . . man? Humanoid? Machine?

"You should be done with this by now."

Ferus spun around in his chair. "Hey, don't you ever say hello?"

"Emperor Palpatine has requested your presence."

Ferus frowned, surprised. "My presence where?"

"He is arriving at the landing platform at the Hall of Ministers in fifteen minutes. Then we are to pro-ceed to the reception hall. Bog Divinian is receiving a tribute from the Samarian ministers of state."

"The Emperor is coming here? Why?" Palpatine rarely left Coruscant now.

"That is not for you to question. Be there." Vader stalked out.

"Nice to see you, too," Ferus muttered under his breath.

Darth Vader was in charge of all of the Empire's operations on Samaria, which meant that he was technically Ferus's boss. Vader treated him with thinly veiled boredom or contempt, depending on his mood. Ferus wasn't insulted. He was happy not to have to pretend to be buddies.

Ferus closed the program he was running on the amazingly tweaked Platform-7 and headed out. The building he was in was part of a vast government complex, so he could walk to the ministers' hall through a series of turbolifts and connecting hallways.

Samaria was a desert planet, and Sath was its major city. In the past century, city planners had created a vast artificial bay that curved around two-thirds of the city. The most exclusive neighborhoods were spread out on a series of land extensions into the bay in a pattern of many-petaled flowers. Government buildings, as well as homes for the wealthy and the palace of the prime minister, were located here.

Ferus noted the extra buzz in the hallways. Some of the ministers, dressed in their sky-blue official robes, were also heading to the landing platform. Although there was a healthy opposition to the Empire in Sath, ministers were canny politicians. They'd curry favor with the Emperor if they had to.

But why had the Emperor asked for his presence at a purely ceremonial affair?

Ferus had let the saboteur of the Sathan computer go, but there was no way for Palpatine to know that.

Or was there?

And why was Palpatine so interested in Samaria? It was a technologically sophisticated planet, true. But Lemurtoo was a small system, with only the neighboring planet of Rosha orbiting the same sun.

The Emperor had told Ferus he wanted to help Samaria thrive . . . but Ferus would believe that the day he believed in space angels.

Ferus hopped on the turbolift to the landing platform. He wanted to be gone. He wanted to return to the asteroid base and see his friends. But for now, he'd better stick around.

He had a feeling his work here wasn't quite done.

CHAPTER TWO

The Legislators' private landing platform was a large one, protruding from the fiftieth floor of the Hall of Ministers. Because it was open to the sky, a cooling system was installed in the overhang in an attempt to regulate the hot, dry climate. The cool air helped, but standing out here for so long was making everyone wilt. Emperor Palpatine was late. No one dared activate the transparisteel canopy bubble, for fear of offending him.

The top ministers ringed the platform. Perched on their shoulders or attached to specially designed holsters were personal droids, all customized with different colors and jeweled insets. All Samarians wore these small, lightweight droids, which had been developed exclusively on the planet from a prototype design from LeisureMech Industries. Each droid had a sleek design that combined the personal-servant features of a luxury droid and the hardwiring of a tech droid. They were about the size of a light-weight mouse droid. Known as Personal Droid Helpers, most Samarians called them PDs, or the more affectionate Peteys.

Samarians didn't use credits. Everything from their taste in tea to the fuel level in their speeders was kept track of by their PDs. All they had to do was walk into a café or fueling station and the purchase would be automatically deleted from a central account. Everything in Samarians' lives was con-tained in their droids, from their transit records to the boot sizes of their children.

Aaren Larker, the prime minister of Samaria, stood waiting, his aide by his side. Bog Divinian, the Imperial advisor, kept near the cooling jets, holding his arms out so that perspiration wouldn't stain his royal-blue tunic.

Across the platform, Darth Vader stood in the hot sun, a black presence that seemed to suck all the air and light into his shiny black boots and hel-met. Was Vader sweltering underneath all that black plastoid and armor? Ferus got a certain amount of pleasure out of the idea.

What *was* under that helmet, anyway? There was not a trace of skin to be seen, nothing to indicate what species Darth Vader was. Humanoid, certainly. Once again Ferus wondered where Vader had come from. If only he knew that, he might hold the key to defeating Palpatine. Or not. At any rate, it would satisfy his curiosity.

At last Ferus glimpsed the flash of the Emperor's personal shuttle. Everyone followed its path as the ship glided downward and landed. Ferus could feel the relief bouncing off the ferrocrete with the heat. After this they could all get back to climate control.

The ramp extended until it touched the ground. The Emperor appeared at the top, his Red Guards behind him. Ferus couldn't see his face. His hood, as usual, covered his scarred and furrowed skin, his yellowed eyes. He held out his arms to the waiting ministers, in the odd greeting Ferus had noted he'd adopted. As though he were so busy gathering in all that worship that he couldn't be bothered to say hello. The ministers bowed in greeting.

The Emperor slowly descended. His head turned to one side, seeing Darth Vader, and then toward Ferus, who could feel the flash of the Emperor's regard. It sent a shiver through him. Ferus could never show how being around him was like being slammed with bad frequencies. He kept his expression neutral as his throat constricted.

Bog Divinian started forward, but the Emperor ignored him. To Ferus's surprise, the Emperor moved instead in Ferus's direction, turning his back on

Vader and leaving Bog looking foolish, striding toward an empty ramp.

If this was intended to demonstrate Ferus's growing influence, Ferus could have done without it. He didn't want to be a rival to Darth Vader. He wanted to keep his head down, gather all the information he could on the Empire, and get out.

The Emperor approached him. The Red Guards stayed a discreet distance away. The ministers hesitantly moved toward the turbolifts. Darth Vader had not moved.

"Ferus Olin, you have done well," the Emperor said. "I asked you to restore Samaria to a functioning power again, and you did so."

"The saboteur escaped." The saboteur had turned out to be Astri Oddo, an old friend of Obi-Wan Kenobi's whom Ferus had known only slightly. He had let her and her son Lune escape with the help of his friends.

"Yes, but that was not your responsibility," the Emperor said with a glance at Darth Vader across the platform. "It belonged to someone else. You did what was required and you did it quickly. Your efficiency has been noted. We value efficiency in the Empire. It can be more valuable than strength."

"Or perhaps it's a necessary component of strength."

"Very true. Now," the Emperor said, turning to

walk toward the turbolift, "come and walk with me. I have something to discuss with you. I'm glad you remained on the planet. It shows respect."

"Or a lack of transport," Ferus observed.

The Emperor ignored this. He wasn't one for jokes. But that didn't mean Ferus didn't derive some pleasure out of launching a few his way. One thing about the Imperials, they were a humorless bunch. "I would like your assessment of the current situation here," Palpatine said.

Ferus clicked into a businesslike mode. "The infrastructure has been restored up to ninety-eight percent and by the end of today will be fully operational —"

"I am not talking about the infrastructure. I am not a bureaucrat. I am interested in your impressions of the situation."

Ferus thought a moment. He knew what the Emperor was asking. "The population was unnerved by the infrastructure crash," Ferus confided. "It left the city feeling vulnerable. Bog Divinian is exploiting the vulnerability. He's hinting that the delegation from Rosha is behind it."

"They are here to negotiate a trade agreement."

"The first ever. The two planets have been technological rivals for decades. Exploiting the Samarian distrust of the Roshans isn't a bad strategy to gain power, but it could backfire. Most Samarians now support trade with Rosha. If they discover that Divinian is manufacturing the charges against the Roshans, the whole thing could blow up in your face. You'd have unrest here, and distrust of the Empire will grow. That would feed the resistance."

"I could simply blame Divinian, and then remove him from office."

"Well, that's a strategy. But the Samarians wouldn't believe you. You'd have to use force to crush the planet." *Which you don't mind doing.*

"What about this resistance?" the Emperor asked. "They have struck a few Imperial targets and have been successful."

"Their numbers are small," Ferus said. He was treading on dangerous ground here. He had remained on the planet to help the resistance. He didn't want to give the Emperor a reason to crack down, but if he minimized their strength too much, the Emperor would become suspicious.

"They seem well organized."

"Yes," Ferus agreed. He had to. Both of the operations to knock out Imperial transports had been executed flawlessly. If he didn't admit that, Palpatine would suspect his involvement.

"You know more about resistance groups than Lord Vader. He wouldn't admit that, but it's true," the Emperor said. By his tone one could almost think he was musing aloud, but Ferus didn't buy it for a minute. This whole conversation had been cal-culated, and Ferus had the feeling the outcome was inevitable. He began to feel nervous. Very nervous.

"Only Sath matters on Samaria," Palpatine con-tinued. "If resistance is crushed here, it will be eliminated planetwide. And here is where the com-puter system crashed. Lord Vader tells me you have not been able to restore the records of any subver-sives on the planet."

"That was the saboteur's first target, it turns out," Ferus said. "Those records are gone forever."

"What the galaxy doesn't understand," Palpatine continued, "is that resistance results in problems for a society as a whole — there is property damage, restricted movement for all, an atmosphere of fear and distrust. The best outcome for this planet is that it continues to be a prosperous, well-run society."

"Of course." There really were times when Ferus felt he was in the middle of a dream. This couldn't be real. He couldn't be walking alongside Emperor Palpatine and *agreeing* with him.

He knew he was being manipulated. He was here to play out the game. He had to seem reluctant, but he also had to seem corruptible. But it had to be a challenge, or Palpatine would suspect him.

"I want you to find the leaders of the resistance cell in Sath and bring them a message," Palpatine went on. "I offer them amnesty, if they disband. We must maintain the peace."

Amazing. Ferus wanted to shake his head at the sheer audacity of it. This figure of evil and destruction claimed to be carrying a message of peace.

"You forget I don't know who the resistance is," Ferus said.

"I forget nothing," Palpatine said, a hint of sharpness in his tone. "That is a minor detail. And who better to bring them the message than one who has been granted amnesty himself?"

There it was. The inevitable trap. Ferus marveled at its cleverness, even as he winced as it bit into him. He had been given amnesty, so they'd trust him. He could reassure them of the Emperor's trustworthiness without saying a word. And then Palpatine would crush them. It might not be now, it might not even be soon, but it would be.

They were steps away from the turbolift. Darth Vader was still standing a hundred meters away, waiting. An Imperial officer stood by the turbolift, ready to activate the sensor. Ferus could see the darkening of his collar as the sweat had rolled down his neck and collected there. Palpatine was making them all wait. He was taking his time.

Palpatine stopped walking and turned to him. Ferus wished he hadn't. It was when he was staring into that ravaged face that he came closest to losing his nerve.

"You do not like to think so, but you're drawn to power," Palpatine told him, inclining his head so that his voice curled around Ferus's ear. "We are just beginning the new era. Make no judgments yet. The climb to power for any government takes some ruthlessness to ensure a just end. Things before were corrupt and breaking down. You must admit that to be true."

"Yes." But how much of that breakdown in stability was due to Palpatine's own maneuvering? Ferus didn't know. Palpatine had cleverly used the greed and corruption of the Senators — and the blindness of the Jedi — to build his power and then make his move.

"I am here to demonstrate that peace and stability in the galaxy are possible only through me." The Emperor looked over the city of Sath below them, at the artificial fingers of sand that stretched out into the aquamarine sea. "You are standing at a cross-roads, Ferus Olin. You should consider where you truly belong. You flourished at the Jedi Temple. You thrived under its rules, its structure. What I am building is much better. A central clearing house in which the politics and stability of the galaxy are acted on by wise minds."

Ferus didn't know what to say, so he said nothing.

Palpatine was drawing him in. It was a clumsy effort. Yes, he had thrived under the rules of the Temple.

But he wasn't that person anymore.

He wasn't crazy about rules anymore. And he definitely didn't like being told what to do.

He would never join the Empire, but it disturbed him that Palpatine seemed to know him intimately. When he spoke of Ferus's life as a Jedi student, he put his finger on exactly how Ferus had experienced it. How could that be? They'd barely had contact. Anakin Skywalker had been Palpatine's favorite, not Ferus.

"Will you do what I have asked?" Palpatine questioned.

"Yes," Ferus said. At least the job would work with his own interest. He could contact the resistance and see what sort of help they might need.

Ferus started to move away, but Palpatine wasn't finished.

"One more thing," the Emperor said. "Contact me directly with your progress reports."

Ferus nodded, trying to keep the surprise off his face. Nobody reported directly to Palpatine except Darth Vader. Ferus had assumed that Vader would be his contact; after all, Vader was in charge of all the Empire's operations on the planet, though he came and went often. Was Palpatine hinting to Ferus that Vader was not quite the favorite he appeared to be?

The Emperor moved off toward Darth Vader, who was still waiting and had not moved a muscle. As Ferus walked toward the turbolift, he could feel Vader's anger like a shove against his back. Ferus hopped onto the turbolift and felt the reassuring movement down toward the planet, away from the heavy Imperial presence.

Another job. He'd never expected that becoming a double agent would happen so fast.

CHAPTER THREE

As soon as Trever reached the secret base, he was ready to leave again. He kicked at the dust — the whole asteroid was just dust and rocks and darkness. Because it didn't orbit a sun, any light came from the upper atmosphere, which was colored by the constantly shifting storm. It made for complete darkness at times, and at others, a dense dark blue or purple haze.

It didn't matter if there was light or not. There was nothing to see.

The base had started with four beings: Ferus, Trever, and Toma and Raina, two resistance commanders who'd been fighting the Empire on their home planet of Acherin. Toma and Raina had hidden Garen Muln during Order 66 and given Ferus his first lead on a surviving Jedi. When Ferus had asked them to run the secret base, they had agreed without hesitation, despite the fact that they had only rudimentary supplies and no ship that could take them away if trouble arrived. They were foes of the Empire and they would work to build the base for any surviving Jedi — the Jedi they all believed in because Ferus believed in them.

Trever was beginning to have his doubts.

They had found two Jedi still alive, so that was something. Solace, who had the most awesome fighting style and the shortest temper Trever had ever seen. Somehow he'd always imagined Jedi as placid and calm, but Solace's moods ranged from grumpy to testy. Garen Muln was a renowned Jedi as well, once a friend to Obi-Wan Kenobi, but he had been so badly wounded that he was no longer capable of much Jedi action. He had even given his lightsaber to Ferus.

Now the group numbered eleven in all. Trever had arrived here with his traveling companions Solace, Oryon, and Clive Fax, and they had sprung two Imperials prisoners — Ferus's best friend, Roan Lands, and their friend Dona, as well as Astri Oddo and her six-year-old son, Lune. They were an odd group with only one thing in common — they were all wanted by the Empire.

They'd commandeered an Imperial ship, a sweet Corellian YT transport, but they'd had to ditch it at a spaceport and find something else. They'd arrived on the asteroid with Solace flying a less impressive and close-to-clunky Class Space Cruiser with a pitted hull and a stripped interior.

They'd arrived to find that conditions had deteriorated. Toma had fallen ill, and though Raina had training as a medic, she lacked the supplies needed to cure him. His recovery was slow, and he was still weak and shaky.

With Toma down, Raina had worked herself to the bone. Garen had tried to help in the greenhouse, but he was still weak, and eventually he pushed himself too far and had to stop. Raina had carried the bulk of the work on her shoulders, and she was in a state of exhaustion by the time they'd returned.

The group had taken stock of the situation and immediately went to work. Solace had barked out orders, and the situation was bad enough that even Clive had obeyed. Oryon had turned out to be a knowledgeable gardener, and he'd recalibrated the soil mix in the greenhouse. Already the plants and vegetables were showing signs of new life. Roan worked on the exterior of the survival pod, which had been buffeted by a strong wind. Clive set to work repairing the landspeeder. Dona foraged for edible plants and set up more vaporators. Astri had helped with Garen and Toma, as well as tweaking the comm system that Toma had managed to set up before he fell ill. Trever himself had helped wherever necessary, which meant he'd spent way too much time pulling weeds and watering in the greenhouse. That would have been bad enough, but he'd also gotten stuck with the most degrading, dirty, despicable job of all — babysitting.

He'd asked Astri if there was something she'd like him to detonate instead, but she'd just grinned and tossed him a lasertoy.

Well, Lune had turned out to be an okay kid. When Ferus had given him that look — the look Trever had come to know so well, the look that meant *do this, do it now, and don't complain* — Trever had taken the boy and escaped from the high-rise building in Sath that had been invaded by stormtroopers. He and Lune had tumbled into Solace's transport, and Astri had gathered Lune into her arms. She hadn't cried, but Trever would never forget the fierceness of her expression or the way she had clasped her son against her. It reminded him of his mother . . . only his mother was dead, so he didn't want to be reminded. He tried not to be around when Astri and Lune were together.

Now he sat outside in a rare moment of light. Occasionally the asteroid would travel by a star system or a sun big enough to penetrate the thick atmosphere, and they would be able to see without glowlights.

He watched as Garen helped Lune keep a ball in the air using the Force. As soon as Garen had seen

Lune, he'd known the boy was Force-sensitive. Those Jedi could sure pick up on whatever that Force thing was. Garen had worked with Lune, helping him "trust his feelings" and "Don't try. Just do." Sure. Whatever the lesson was, it was working. Trever wished he could propel an object just by looking at it. He'd propel plenty of credits his way.

The only person who wasn't tickled by the sight of Garen and Lune was Astri. He saw her watching, and he could feel her worry. Who could blame her? It wasn't exactly a stellar moment to be a Jedi.

He knew that Astri's husband, Bog Divinian, had connived to get Lune away from her. He wanted to enroll Lune in some sort of academy the Empire was starting on Coruscant. He knew Lune was Force-sensitive, so he figured he'd make a hotshot pilot eventually.

Ferus had foiled that plot. But Astri kept on worrying.

Trever tucked his hands around his knees and leaned against a flat boulder. It was the end of a long day. Soon, the others would leave their jobs and gather. Someone would bring a tray with tea. They would sit and report on their progress. Trever didn't know how the routine had been established, but it had. It made them all feel part of something.

Clive arrived first, settling himself next to Trever with an *oof*. "Leave it to Ferus," he said. "If there's an unspeakably dreadful patch of rock you can land a starship on, he'll find it."

It was a variation of what he said every day. Clive was meant for cities and teeming worlds with traffic and restaurants and dangerous characters. He'd once been a double agent during the Clone Wars, as well as a musician and industrial spy. There didn't seem to be anything he couldn't do.

With another sigh, Clive stretched out full-length on the ground. His black hair was filmy with dust, and grease had settled into every crease in his tunic. He was still working on the balky landspeeder. He appeared to be in a state of utter exhaustion, but when Astri walked over and placed her folding stool next to Trever, Clive sat up.

"At least we get some light today," Astri observed. "We must be passing by a big star system."

"Great. More light to see more dust," Clive said.

"What do you expect from a hideout, Clive?" Astri asked. "Fine hotels and sunshine every day?"

"I don't see why not. I've hidden out in many a fine hotel in my day." Clive settled his head back on the rock he'd used as a pillow. "Ferus just has to make things hard. And may I point out that he isn't even here?"

The others began to straggle toward them. Dona appeared, carrying a basket with the bread she'd managed to bake every day despite her other chores.

She loved to feed them, and Toma and Garen already had grown stronger under the spell of her soups and breads. Behind her, Roan carried a small table, which he placed near Trever and the others. Dona laid the basket on it. Then she put her thick, broad hands on her back and stretched.

"A long day's work," she said. "It feels good."

A groan emerged from Clive. "If you say so, mate."

Roan gave him a nudge with his foot and dropped a thick chunk of bread on his chest. "Maybe this will revive you." Like Ferus, Roan had known Clive for years. Roan and Ferus had been partners in the firm of Olin/Lands, which had created new identities for those trying to escape criminal gangs, pirates, or governments — anyone who had crossed an evil organization and needed to hide. Clive had been more of a con man than a whistle-blower, but Ferus and Roan had liked him and helped him anyway. They'd rescued him from several scrapes and earned his loyalty. Clive claimed not to believe in anything but credits in his account, but he was loyal to his friends.

Oryon and Solace joined the group. They were the unofficial leaders. Oryon was a strong, tall Bothan who'd run a successful spy network during the Clone Wars. The Empire had put a price on his head, and he was forced to disappear, joining a group called the Erased on Coruscant. Now he sipped his tea and stood talking quietly with Solace.

"Good news," Oryon said to the others. "Astri was able to fix the comm system today. Toma's got the stormtracker working, so we were able to get a message through to Coruscant. Keets and Curran are out of danger and hiding with Dex. They're driving Dex crazy, but they're safe."

"Glad to hear that," Roan said. "Good work, Astri."

Keets Freely and Curran Caladian were other members of the Erased. They'd risked their necks by returning to Coruscant to gather information, and had almost gotten arrested. Trever was glad to hear they were safe. He wished he was with them, hiding in the Orange District in the sublevels of Coruscant. Sure, it was dangerous, but at least it was lively.

Dona handed Trever a mug of hot tea. He sipped it gratefully. There were enough warming units to go around, but the chill of the asteroid settled in his bones.

Garen and Lune left their game and came over, Lune running to Astri, who spread honey on his piece of bread. Lune chomped on it happily.

The last to join them were Raina and Toma. Toma had grown a beard since his illness, and it was now streaked with gray. He moved with the careful attention of someone who had been recently ill.

Raina was carrying two stools under her arm. She put one down for Toma and motioned to Dona to take the other. She found a flat rock to perch on and accepted a mug from Astri.

Raina flipped her thick auburn braid over her shoulder. "Toma has news," she said.

They all turned to Toma. He wrapped his hands around his mug and leaned forward. "Thanks to Astri's good work," he said, nodding at her, "I've been able to contact someone I knew in the resistance on our homeworld," he said. "Has anyone ever heard of Moonstrike?"

"A moonstrike is when a satellite moon gets hit by an asteroid big enough to give it a wobble in orbit," Oryon said. "It can alter planetary tidal patterns and influence severe weather changes."

"That's what it is," Toma said. "And it is also the name of a secret organization. This contact is the head of it. Her name is Flame. She was an extremely wealthy aristocrat on Acherin when the Empire took over the government. Her family ran the biggest factories and corporations on the planet. She was able to get most of her wealth out before the Empire took over the main industries. Now she's using that wealth to fund Moonstrike. It's her idea to go from planet to planet, contacting any resistance movements. She'll use what she has to fund them and raise more funds through her contacts. The point is organization. We can accomplish so much more if we're in contact. She's put her personal fortune on the line."

"What does this have to do with us?" Clive asked.

"I've just learned that she's on her way to Samaria," Toma said. "This could be helpful to Ferus. Unfortunately we were cut off and I didn't get a chance to tell her about him. But a linking of resistance movements could only help any surviving Jedi. They could move about the galaxy, relying on safe havens. They wouldn't be stuck hiding out on this asteroid."

"It's a plan," Oryon said cautiously. "But the more people know about the Jedi, the more danger it puts them in."

"We have to worry about the safety of the Jedi we haven't found yet," Solace said with a glance at Garen.

"There are only three of you that I know of at the moment," Clive said. "It's not as though there's a Jedi army out there that we need to hide."

Trever looked at the others. Only a few of them knew that Obi-Wan Kenobi was still alive. It was a secret they all would keep.

Garen gave a small smile. "I'd say two and a half Jedi, actually. I'm not worth much these days."

"You are worth far more than you realize," Solace said in the gentlest tone Trever had ever heard her use.

"In any case, Ferus should be aware that Flame is there and will try to make contact with the resistance," Raina said. "Ferus is there to help them."

"One of us should go to Samaria," Oryon said.

"I'll go," Solace said.

Oryon shook his head. "You shouldn't. You're too conspicuous. You were just there, and the Empire is on the lookout for you. I'll go."

"And you're not conspicuous?" Solace asked.

"I'll go," Clive said. "I can't wait to get off this rock, anyway."

"Wait a second, if anyone goes, it should be me," Roan said. "I have the most experience with resistance movements."

"You just escaped from an Imperial prison," Oryon said. "You don't have any ID docs. You can't go."

"I can create a false ID doc in no time."

Toma held up a hand. "This shouldn't be cause for argument. We need to decide on the best person."

"I've done an atmospheric scan," Roan said. "The storms will lessen in severity in five hours. A good time to take off. I say we get some rest, then decide."

The others agreed to this. Everyone headed back to the shelters. Trever walked back slowly. He hadn't said a word, because he knew the others would disagree.

He should be the one to go.

He was the least conspicuous. Nobody paid attention to kids. He knew resistance movements almost as well as Roan. He was a good pilot and a better fighter. He could be useful. The only reason he hadn't stayed in the first place was that Ferus had practically kicked him off the planet.

What really bugged him was that nobody worried about Ferus. Everybody just assumed Ferus was okay. They'd left him on a half-built high-rise, hundreds of meters in the air, surrounded by stormtroopers and wicked droids that could cut through a ship's engine in seconds — not to mention Darth Vader waiting below like some mammoth reclumi spider — and they thought because he was such a great Jedi hotshot, he'd be fine.

Well, Trever had news for all of them: Ferus wasn't a Jedi. He had done some amazing things, no question about it. But Trever had also seen how he'd struggled. He'd seen him make mistakes.

Ferus was no match for Darth Vader.

Ferus needed help.

Trever waited until he heard only even breathing around him. He stole out of the shelter and made his way swiftly to the one transport. He sat in the pilot seat, gathering his courage. Trever had made the journey several times, and although he said he was used to it, the truth was that every time he had to fly through the storm, he was a little bit terrified. He was always glad when they made it through.

But he'd seen Ferus fly through this storm. Solace had just done it. He could do it, too.

He fired up the engines and shot up into the atmosphere. Once he reached the outer atmosphere, the ship immediately began to buck and almost went into a roll. Trever tasted the sourness of fear in his mouth. He righted the ship, remembering to track the currents on the computer and steer with them instead of against them. He could do this.

A trough of low pressure sent him spinning into a vortex of stars. Trever fought for control, his hands slipping from perspiration. He leaned into the ship's dive, fighting the urge to correct it. He let the ship go. With a great shudder, it straightened.

Okay, it wouldn't be easy. But he would do it. He had to.

CHAPTER FOUR

The grand reception room at the Hall of Ministers was a fifty-story lobby, a soaring structure fashioned from arching struts and slender beams. Pale-rose synthstone walls met a blue tiled floor the exact color of the artificial sea glimpsed out of the tall windows. In the center of the room was a circular platform with a repulsorlift motor.

Ferus tried to stay in the back of the crowd, but the Emperor signaled to him, and he found himself standing next to Darth Vader on the platform. Exactly where he didn't want to be.

Slowly, the platform rose in the air and hovered about a meter above the floor. Since this was a political gathering, Ferus prepared himself for one long stretch of boredom. These ceremonies could last longer than a Bespin sunset.

He saw the delegation from Rosha at the very back of the crowd. Roshans were tall, with four antennae as delicate as tendrils and sensitive to light, shrinking back against their heads during the day and unfurling in darkness or with anxiety. Most of them had light eyes of blue or green, and strong, flexible bodies. He was surprised they'd shown up at all, considering all the lies Bog Divinian was spreading about them. Bog had made it sound as if Larker's support of trade between the old rivals was a big mistake.

Ferus's opinion was that Bog was a dim-witted, conniving dolt, but he had to reluctantly admit that he was clever about trying to win over the population. Bog had taken credit for fixing the computer virus that had paralyzed Sathan society, and never stopped praising the planet and its citizens. The Sathans were won over with flattery and given a reason to despise a rival, and that was an irresistible combination.

Aaren Larker, the prime minister of Samaria, gave a short speech thanking the ministers for attending. It was clear the man was pained to have to praise Bog Divinian. All he wanted to do was kick the Empire off his planet.

Ferus wondered how long Larker would last. Already there were calls for a vote of no confidence. He was sure Bog was behind the movement to remove Larker. When he'd arrived on the planet, he thought Bog was foolish to expect that he could rule

Samaria. Now he saw that Bog hadn't been overconfident in the least.

"And now we come to the reason we are here," Larker said. "Due to the unanimous vote of the ministers, I would like to present the Award of the City of Sath to our Imperial advisor, Bog Divinian, who aided us so capably during the crisis. To show our appreciation, we bestow upon him this gift of his own personal droid, manufactured here on Samaria."

Ferus watched Bog's smile broaden. He probably wasn't quick-witted enough to realize that Larker had called him only "capable." That was hardly high praise.

Yet here was Bog, acknowledging the applause, smiling broadly and stepping forward. Larker handed over a personal droid, which Bog plopped on his shoulder as if he'd been doing that all his life, giving it a small pat that sent the ministers into more applause.

"You know, I always wanted one of these fellows," Bog said. "My very own Petey! I'm hoping he's going to reform me. Get me to meetings on time."

A chuckle ran through the ministers.

"Better yet, maybe he'll tell me when to take a break!"

Scattered claps and a great hoot of laughter from the ministers. Bog was working the crowd.

"But seriously . . ." Bog paused to let the noise die down. "I've only been here for a few months, but I feel like I've lived here all my life. You Samarians, you work hard, you play hard, and you make things happen. Now, other planets might have a hard time with that —" Bog held up a hand as murmuring swept through the audience. It was an obvious reference to Rosha. Larker frowned and looked as though he wanted to shove Bog off the repulsorlift platform. "— but the Empire doesn't. Some other planets might want to bring you down, make themselves feel smarter. I'll tell you this — it's not going to happen. Because Samarians always win!"

Cheers rose from the ministers. Ferus couldn't believe they were buying this. Bog was making interplanetary relations seem like a Podrace.

"And that's why —" Another pat for the personal droid on his shoulder. "— I'm proud to be an honorary Samarian!"

The hall went wild. The ministers pushed forward as the platform lowered, all anxious to shake Bog's hand. The HoloNet cameras zoomed in as reporters began to talk excitedly about Bog.

Ferus saw Vader move closer to the Emperor. Using his old Jedi training, he screened out the noise around him and honed in on only two voices.

"He was promoted beyond his competence, we thought," Palpatine said. "But look at him."

"He is a fool," Darth Vader said.

"Yes," Palpatine admitted. "He is exactly what we need."

Ferus milled among the crowd, trying to pick up what the mood was. It was apparent that the ministers had been swept along in the tide of Bog's self-regard. Bog's speech had moved through the city like wildfire, and the HoloNet on the planet was rebroadcasting it to cheers at every gathering place in Sath.

He noted how the ministers flocked around Bog but left the prime minister of Samaria by himself. Ferus moved toward him. He had been waiting for days to get Larker alone.

"Do you hear them?" Larker said to him. "They are transferring their loyalty to an Imperial advisor. Which I suppose makes you happy."

"Not particularly."

"You're one of them."

"No. I did a job for them. There's a difference."

Larker gave him a long look. "Keep telling yourself that," he said softly.

"I know that you hired Astri Oddo to sabotage the computers," Ferus said quietly. "I arranged for her escape. She must have contacted you."

"She did."

"Then you know you can trust me."

Larker's gaze roamed the crowd. "I can't trust anyone."

"If Bog continues to whip the city into a frenzy about the Roshan threat, you can step forward and admit it was you who gave the order to sabotage the computers, not the Roshans."

"And if I do that, I'll be arrested, and Bog will become governor," Larker said.

"You might not have a choice," Ferus said. "Bog is lining up support among the ministers to oust you."

"They won't betray me, in the end," Larker said. "I've been working on establishing this agreement with the Roshans for years. The ministers all support it. The time to keep industrial secrets is over. We are each technological innovators, but if we work together we can make even bigger strides. We are experts in macrotechnology — we can run cities, planets with our systems. They have made enormous strides in microtechnology. Their droids are among the smallest in the galaxy, with the most sophisticated systems. We had a setback when Rosha sided with the Separatists during the Clone Wars. They were deeply involved with the Trade Federation. But they've come to regret it. Now we can achieve a real trade agreement. We can share our technology."

"Not if the Empire has anything to say about it."

"They don't. They don't interfere in systemwide

trade agreements. They don't want the galactic economy to crash."

"No, they just want to control it. Why do you think Bog is so against the trade agreement?"

Larker shrugged. "Because I support it. That's reason enough. He knows that the average Samarian fears the Roshans, so he'll use it as a wedge to gain support." He gave Ferus a searching look. "You say you're just a contract worker, working for credits. You know something about me that could bring me down, yet you don't use it. Why?"

"Because I'm on your side. And I could use your help. The Emperor has asked me to find the resistance and offer them amnesty if they disband."

Larker looked at him sharply. "And you expect them to do this?"

"No. But I was hired to deliver the message personally. If I can find them and talk to them, I might be able to help them. I was one of the founding members of the resistance on Bellassa. We struck many blows against the Empire after it took over the government. The city rose against them."

"But the Empire is still in control."

"You can't kick the Empire off your planet. You can only make it hard for them to control you. And you wait for better opportunities."

"So," Larker said, "you were one of the founders

of the Eleven, and yet here you are. Were you offered amnesty by the Emperor, too?"

"Yes."

Larker looked at him with contempt. "So you took it and abandoned your cause."

"Not exactly," Ferus said. He couldn't explain fully. It would compromise his mission. "I am still working for the cause, but . . . in a different way."

But it was too late. He'd lost Larker.

"I can't help you," Larker said. "I don't know anything about the resistance, anyway."

Just then the assistant who'd been lurking nearby approached. Larker seized on the interruption. "Yes, Dahl?"

"The Roshan delegation would like to speak with you. Robbyn Sark especially is anxious to go over some details of the agreement."

"Of course." Larker nodded at Ferus and started across the crowded floor. Ferus watched as he said a few words into the aide's ear. Dahl nodded.

A shadow fell across the tiles, and Darth Vader appeared next to Ferus.

"You had a long conversation," Vader calmly observed.

"He's a chatty guy."

"Do not forget who you are working for. Larker is not to be trusted."

"The way I see it, nobody is to be trusted around here. But thanks for the warning."

"The Emperor gave you an assignment. I expect a full briefing."

"You can expect it, but you won't be getting it." Ferus was beginning to enjoy himself. "The Emperor's instruction was to report to him directly on my progress. No one else. And that would include you."

Vader said nothing for a moment. Ferus only heard the rasp of his automated, eerie breathing.

Then Darth Vader abruptly turned and strode away. His meaning was all too clear to Ferus: *I'm going to enjoy destroying you.*

Oops. Ferus had tried to keep out of Vader's way. He really had. But apparently he hadn't succeeded.

Ferus waited outside the Hall of Ministers. He rested against the platform of a large sculpture, slabs of stone and chunks of plastoid and quadrillum that were supposed to represent a gigantic version of a droid's sensor suite. More than anything, the Samarians worshipped technology. He didn't think much of the sculpture, but it hid him from notice and gave him a clear view of the huge double doors of the exit.

After only a moment or two, Larker's aide, Dahl, walked out the door and briskly through the front gates. Air taxis patrolled this area of Sath, busily whisking ministers from one government building to another. Dahl activated the blinking search signal on his personal droid, the method Sathans used to hail air taxis. A vehicle pulled up immediately.

Ferus hailed his own taxi the old-fashioned way — he held up his hand.

His driver followed the taxi in front without a question. The taxi ahead soared through the traffic lanes in no hurry and with no attempt to lose a tail. Obviously Dahl had no idea he was being followed and took no precautions. That was odd. Perhaps Ferus had read the situation wrong. He had assumed that Dahl was Larker's liaison to the resistance, but if that were so, Ferus would have expected him to take evasive action routinely.

The air taxi stopped at a café and Dahl hopped out.

Well. Ferus would either get a lead on the resistance, or lunch.

Ferus had his own taxi pull up a block ahead. He followed the ramp back to the café. He tracked Dahl as he moved through the crowd. Dahl headed toward the back, where Sathans were ordering food and drinks at a service bar. Keeping out of sight in case Dahl looked back, Ferus drifted off to the right. Dahl joined the line.

Suddenly a young woman behind Ferus stepped back into a waiter, who dropped the tray full of empty glasses he was holding. The glasses crashed to the floor. Ferus quickly melted back in case Dahl turned, as everyone else in the café did.

But Dahl didn't turn. He slipped through the crowd and disappeared.

Swiftly Ferus turned back and headed for the front entrance. He had no doubt that Dahl had gone out a back exit.

A classic move. Use the distraction to lose the tail, if it was there. Dahl was just being careful. Ferus exited, making sure there was no one behind him. He turned down a side street and Force-leaped up to the roof of the building, landing without a sound. He ran lightly across the roof. Looking down, he could see Dahl quickly heading down a back street, checking behind him to make sure no one was there.

Leaping from rooftop to rooftop, Ferus was able to keep Dahl in sight as he moved through the climate-controlled walkways that crisscrossed all the city levels in Sath. At last he turned into a Speeder Exchange, a large lot where used airspeeders were for sale. Dahl moved from one speeder to the next, appearing to consider them.

Ferus leaped down into an alley that connected to the lot. From here he had a perfect vantage point.

A salesman drifted over, but Dahl shook his head and walked away. Dahl slipped into a yellow speeder, checking out the controls casually. Then he jumped out again, checked out a few more speeders, and left.

Ferus had seen what he'd come to see. He'd just witnessed a drop. He let Dahl disappear down the street. He waited.

In another moment, the curly-haired young woman who'd caused the distraction at the café entered the lot. She smiled at the salesman, walked through the lot examining different vehicles, and climbed into the yellow speeder. She put her hands on the controls and examined the dashboard.

She got out, shrugged at the salesman, waved, and continued down the street. Her personal droid was a metallic red, and her tunic was snug-fitting and reached down to her black boots. She was dressed as a typical stylish young Sathan.

And she was in the resistance.

Ferus followed her by the same method, leaping from roof to roof and occasionally, if there were good sight lines, from the walkway one level above. He was good at this. Skills he had learned as a Jedi had been honed as he worked in his own business, and later as a member of the resistance on Bellassa.

The woman entered a small cantina. Ferus waited a few minutes, then strolled inside. The woman sat at a table in the back. An older man had joined her. Ferus took a seat at the bar.

He considered his next move. The most direct was most likely best. He would just approach them.

He was about to get up when he felt something small and cold nudge him in the back.

"Yeah, it's a blaster," a deep voice said. "So don't make a move. I'd like a word with you in the alley."

CHAPTER SIX

Trever had thought he could handle just about anything the galaxy could throw at him at this point, but he'd barely made it through the storm, and the ship was failing as it approached Samaria. He had the coordinates where Flame would be — thanks to a quick search of Toma's private database — but he had about two more minutes before he lost his engines and crashed.

Maybe it hadn't been the brightest idea to take off like that.

Well. At this point he had nothing to lose. He'd either be space dust or he'd succeed in landing and finding Flame . . . and Ferus. Trever gritted his teeth and kept his hands on the sweat-slicked controls. The craft was a bit out of control now. His plan was to come in fast and hug the ground in the hopes of evading any Imperial tracking sensors. Technically, Trever was supposed to check in and land at the main landing platform in Sath, but rules made him itchy, and Imperials made him break out in hives.

When he hadn't been worrying on the journey, he'd been checking out the nav database. The area he was supposed to land in lay outside Sath. Samaria had vast areas of wilderness, and the Crystal Forest was one of them. Although it was a popular destination for tourists and campers, much of it was still wild.

The Crystal Forest had formed millions of years before, when the planet was an ice planet. Crystals had formed cliffs and treelike shapes that towered hundreds of meters high. It was supposed to be an inspiring sight, but all Trever cared about was that it would provide good cover.

Suddenly, as Trever gripped the controls of the failing ship, he saw the area below. It looked like a red haze at first, but as he approached he was able to differentiate the gnarled massive forms in tones of rust and orange and gold that rose from the planet's surface. It was oddly and eerily beautiful.

The ship shuddered and groaned, then heeled to starboard. Trever had to push the failing engines to avoid slamming into one of the towering shapes. Now he was in the thick of it, the ship with its screaming engines lurching and stalling as he desperately looked for somewhere to land.

This place had seemed so galactically cool from

the relative safety of the atmosphere. But the tree-like forms weren't so cool when you were heading straight toward them. This place had its own weather system, too. Winds howled through the canyons created by the formations, slammed against the ship, and caused Trever to scream out loud when metal shrieked from the impact of a sharp crystal scraping along the side.

He had to bring the ship down. He had to do it or he would die.

Desperately searching now, Trever descended. One wing of the ship bashed into a crystal formation, and more red lights suddenly blinked insistently on the control panel.

"Just hold on," Trever muttered.

Coming up fast on his right, he saw a small clear space on the surface. He remembered a trick of Ferus's. He cut the engines, turned hard right, crossed his fingers, let out a howl of desperation, and held on as the ship shuddered, creaked, and then dropped like a stone into the opening.

Trever felt his body fly up with the impact. His teeth slammed into his lower lip. He heard a horrible tearing noise and the ship made a quarter turn, then stopped. With a gasp, the engines died.

Trever, however, was still alive. He thought.

It took him several minutes to be able to move.

His body shook from the effort it took. With trembling fingers he dabbed at the blood on his lip with the hem of his tunic.

"Get a grip. You're safe." He said the words out loud. He was embarrassed that he'd been in such a state of terror. He'd been through a lot in the past month or so with Ferus. He'd thought he was brave. He'd never realized how much of his bravery he had borrowed from Ferus.

He raised himself from the chair and looked around. The ship had basically collapsed around him. The cockpit was intact, but he could have trouble exiting if the ramp didn't work.

He pressed the release. To his relief, it squeaked open. It didn't slide all the way down, but that wasn't a problem. He wiggled to the top and jumped. The forest floor was like transparisteel, smooth and cold.

Flame had given Toma the coordinates where she would land and said she'd wait there for at least two hours, in hopes that Toma could send someone to meet her. The two hours were up about a half hour ago, but Trever hoped she hadn't given up yet. He got his bearings on his datapad map and struck out for the coordinates.

Although the surface temp readout on the ship had prepared him for heat, the hard crystal formations and the forest floor radiated coolness into the air. Trever kept up a good pace. The place was quiet. No forest creatures could live in this environment; there was no vegetation, no water. Trever hoped he'd bump into Flame soon. This place was starting to spook him out.

Suddenly the quiet was broken by a soft whirring he recognized as a speeder engine. Trever wanted to rush forward but he had learned caution on Bellassa. He slipped behind one of the formations and waited.

Two airspeeders zoomed out from between the formations. Imperial stormtroopers, four in each vehicle. He could tell they were tracking someone. They made a hard right and streaked off.

After another moment he heard another speeder. He flattened himself against the crystal, feeling the points against his back.

The silver speeder flew by, going at top speed. He had only a flash of an impression, a figure in a black flight suit with a shiny black helmet.

It had to be Flame.

Trever had to take the chance. He stepped out from behind the crystal formation and tried to signal the speeder with the glowlight from his utility belt.

He was too late. The speeder took a sharp turn around a gnarled crystal ten meters wide and disappeared.

Trever sprang back toward the rock, but the

Imperial speeders had circled back and he was too late. He made a dash for cover, but one of the Imperial speeders peeled off — and came straight for him.

He'd been spotted.

CHAPTER SEVEN

Ferus faced the alley wall. The blaster was held right at the tender part of his neck, and his companion wasn't shy about pressing the barrel hard into his flesh.

"Do you think we're stupid?" his assailant asked.

"Who's we?"

The barrel was pushed even deeper. Ferus tried not to wince. He was getting annoyed. He knew he could disarm whoever it was behind him in seconds, but he also knew that aggression at this point wouldn't get him what he wanted.

"Do you think we're stupid?" the assailant repeated.

"No. I don't think you're stupid. A little short on manners, maybe. But if I thought you were stupid, I wouldn't be here trying to find you."

"So you admit you're trying to find us." The

barrel angled toward Ferus's head. "You are an agent of the Empire."

"Well," Ferus said, "technically, that's true. I guess that sounds bad. But it doesn't mean I can't help you."

The assailant gave an incredulous laugh. "I should just shoot you now."

"But then you wouldn't find out what I came to say. Why don't you hear me out, and then shoot me if you want to?"

"Because I don't have time to waste."

Ferus could feel that despite his tough talk, his assailant didn't want to shoot him. He wasn't dealing with a hardened killer.

"Look, this might go easier if I introduced myself."

"I know who you are. Ferus Olin."

"I was one of the founding members of the Eleven on Bellassa."

"I've heard of Ferus Olin. But I've never seen him."

"So you think I'm an impostor?"

"I think the Empire is capable of anything. I was warned about you."

"By Dahl. Larker's aide. I saw the drop."

He heard his assailant suck in air through his teeth. "Larker only helps us from time to time. He's not one of us. And he doesn't know Bellassa like I do. The real Ferus Olin could be trusted. The real Ferus Olin wouldn't work for the Emperor."

"Things change. Listen, I'm just a contract employee. Think about it. What better way to find out how the Empire works than by working for them?"

"Are you saying you're a double agent?"

"Now you're catching on."

There was a pause. "What's the location of the safehouse of the Eleven?"

"Aw, c'mon. That's a stupid test."

The barrel pressed into his flesh again.

"Okay, okay, not stupid . . . uh, not helpful? You know I can't tell you that, even with a blaster at my head. Ask me something else."

"What was the first job the Eleven did together?"

Ferus thought about this. He knew the answer. The Eleven — back when there really were only eleven members — had broken into Imperial files and discovered the names of the Imperial spies who had infiltrated the capital city of Ussa. The raid was still a secret kept by the original group, because jobs were never discussed unless they had to be. If his assailant knew someone on the inside who had told him, Ferus could corroborate the information. It didn't matter, at this point — the Imperial spies had long ago been rotated to other assignments.

"A raid on the Imperial files at the garrison head-quarters to discover the names of Imperial spies."

"How many spies did you discover?"

"Four."

The pressure on his head lessened. "You can turn around."

Ferus turned. His assailant was younger than he'd thought, maybe a few years older than Trever. His deep, gritty voice rose from a thick, muscular chest. Thick brown hair brushed the collar of his tunic. He still held the blaster.

"How did you know that was the truth?" Ferus asked.

"I knew someone who was close to the group," he said. "When we started the resistance here, I went to Ussa and a few other planets to see if I could study a successful operation. I was able to get some strategy tips. Someone was kind enough to brief me on the first job."

"Dr. Amie Antin," Ferus said. "That's who you know."

"How do you know?"

"Because you said your contact was close to the group, but not in the group. Amie wasn't at that time. But she treated Wil after the raid — he had a small fracture in his wrist. So she knew about it."

"Good deduction. I'm Dinko, by the way. Code name. We all use them — it's better if we don't know anyone's real name." The young man grinned, transforming his features from forbidding to welcoming. "I guess I should say welcome to the Samarian resistance."

Ferus rubbed his neck. "You sure know how to make a guy feel welcome."

Suddenly the grin on Dinko's face faded. "I haven't heard from Amie in several weeks. We were in close contact. Do you know anything?"

"They had to move the base of operations after Roan was arrested. There was a crackdown. I hear they had to disband for a time."

"We don't want what happened there to happen here, that's for sure," Dinko said. "Come on, meet the others."

Ferus followed him back into the cantina. Dinko walked directly to the table with the curly-haired young woman and the older man. "This is Nek and Firefolk," he said.

He turned to the ethereal young woman with the reddish curls. "I think I've met Firefolk before," he said.

She grinned. "Try again. I'm Nek."

"I'm Firefolk," the man with the silver hair said.

"Sorry." Ferus was amused at the idea of the sweet-faced young woman taking one of the more hideous species in the galaxy, the nek battle dog, as her code name. He would have guessed she would have chosen the more fanciful Firefolk — tiny, glowing beings native to the forest moon of Endor. He sat down.

"First let me tell you why I'm officially here," he said. "Emperor Palpatine has an offer on the table. He will grant you amnesty if you disband."

"This is good news," the silver-haired Firefolk said. "It means we're getting to them."

"The Emperor offered me amnesty, and I took it," Ferus said. "It was a way to get inside. It's something to consider."

"It's a way to get arrested," Dinko said. "I don't trust it."

"You shouldn't," Ferus said.

"All right, you passed along the message," Firefolk said. "We refuse. Now, let's move on."

"Ferus wants to help us," Dinko said.

"So far the Empire hasn't taken over your government," Ferus said. "I think it's because the Emperor is still trying to consolidate power, and he doesn't want to give any other planets a reason to resent him. He's going to try to influence governments, not take them over. Willing governments will get governors. I've seen it happen on some of the Core Worlds. When the Empire tried to install a governor on Bellassa, we revolted, and that's when they came in with a battalion and took over. You don't want that to happen."

"So that's why they sent Divinian here," Dinko said. "They call him an advisor, but he's trying to get elected."

Ferus nodded. "Samarians don't exclude outlanders from becoming prime minister, so he has a way in. Bog is gaining power. It will be a good thing for the Imperials if he's actually elected. They can use him to point out to other planets that they mean no harm."

"And meanwhile, the Sathans just let it happen," Dinko said darkly. "We're going to let our enemy walk right in. We'll even pull up a chair for him."

"The population is afraid," Firefolk said. "Afraid of losing what we have."

"As long as someone promises they'll keep their personal droids and their comfortable life, they'll believe anything," Nek added.

"I'm afraid Bog is winning this game," Ferus said. "He's mustered up the support to call for a vote of no-confidence for Larker."

"He's bribing the ministers," Nek said.

"If you had proof of that, it could be helpful," Ferus said. "The Emperor is still concerned with appearances. He might recall Bog back to Coruscant. But at the very least, it would expose what he's doing and he'd lose support here."

Nek, Firefolk, and Dinko exchanged glances.

"We could get the proof," Dinko said. "If all goes well."

"How?"

"Do you know that the ministers gave Bog a gift of a personal droid?"

"I was at the ceremony."

"An operative working for us programmed Bog's PD. He placed a chip in it that allows us to monitor his communications. We expect to have the proof, possibly within hours, maybe in a day . . . but we're sure we'll have it. That droid will record every communication, every transaction that Bog makes."

"Good. Bog isn't your only problem, but he's the biggest one at the moment. It will take the Empire awhile to replace him. In the meantime, Larker can consolidate his power and you can recruit more members."

"If we get rid of Bog, it will convince Sathans that we're worth joining," Dinko said.

"I'll report back to the Emperor that you're considering his offer," Ferus said. "In the meantime, it would be helpful if I could bring him something that will convince him I'm on his side. Do you have a drop you don't use anymore that I can tell him about?"

"How about the speeder place?" Nek suggested. "We've used it for a month now. It's time to find a new place for a drop."

"Good." Ferus stood. "How can I contact you again?"

"Do you know the Twilight Fountain on Talo Square?"

Ferus nodded. He had committed most of Sath to memory by now.

"If you go there at midday, we'll contact you. Otherwise in case of emergency we can use com-links. We have to keep messages short in case the Empire is monitoring," Dinko said.

"Good policy." Ferus nodded a good-bye.

He walked out, feeling a strange reluctance to leave. It wasn't only that this group reminded him of his time with the Eleven. It was a feeling that they were in danger, becoming involved in something so big that they couldn't possibly win.

He'd heard the Emperor's words. Palpatine spoke of letting the planet govern itself — but if Bog failed to take over, would the Empire just call in troops for an invasion? He didn't know.

He just hoped that whatever the Empire was planning, the resistance could survive it.

CHAPTER EIGHT

The situation on Samaria was not unmanageable, Darth Vader thought. It wasn't even terribly difficult. Even that fool, Bog Divinian, was managing to manipulate popular opinion. Taking over the planet would be as easy as slicing through durasteel with a lightsaber.

So if things were under control, why was he still here? He had a galaxy to manage. Even while he'd been here, reports continued to flow in from other planets. There were plenty of matters he had to keep a hand in. Some could be handled easily with a threat or a directive. Others merited a personal visit. But his Master wanted him here, for now.

In just a few days, he'd brought the military chief in line. The battalion was secretly orbiting the Lemurtoo system, ready to be called in on a moment's notice. The captain of the battalion had drawn up a plan to guard the spaceport and station troops around the city. He was agitating to move in. Vader had quickly vetoed that ridiculous plan. It was just an attempt from a lesser military mind to thrust himself into importance. He'd ordered the battalion to stay hidden until they were needed. If they had to stage a coup, they would, but it would be done quickly. Stationing troops without needing to was foolish. It just fanned the flames of resistance.

So what was bothering him? Vader turned to survey the government buildings that rose out of the petaled extensions of land that the Sathans had constructed in an aquamarine sea. He knew what was bothering him, he just didn't want to name it.

Ferus Olin.

Reporting directly to the Emperor.

Why hadn't Olin left after restoring Platform-7? He'd been given amnesty. He could have taken off. Yet he'd stayed. And when the Emperor had arrived, he had singled Olin out.

Darth Vader wasn't about to succumb to petty jealousy. Those emotions were gone forever, as foreign to him as love. He had felt love once. He had failed at it. So he had turned his mind and his power to other things. What remained had distilled down to a pureness he relished. Duty. A job to fulfill. Power to grab and consolidate and protect, and a Master to serve.

It was like this body armor he wore, this

life-sustaining suit. In the beginning, he'd felt trapped by it. But he'd learned to use it for both intimidation and isolation. It allowed him to feel separate from all the beings around him, and that turned out to be very useful.

Do you see me now, Obi-Wan? I'm not connecting to the Living Force. I am looking at it from a distance. It can't touch me now.

You were wrong, my old Master. I don't need to connect to it. I just need to control it.

Vader turned away from the sight of the sea. He pushed away the thought of his former Master, as he always did. Thoughts and memories of the past came less frequently now.

Until Ferus Olin had shown up.

Jealousy wasn't an option for him anymore, but analysis was. He was adept at manipulation, at figuring out motives, of thinking ten steps ahead of anyone else. But Olin . . . he couldn't figure him out. If he was a double agent, he was a fool. He wasn't going to learn anything. He wasn't going to make a difference.

Could he truly be half fascinated by the power he saw? Could he be turned to the dark side? That's what his Master thought. That could be the only reason his Master was taking an interest.

Could his Master be right? The dark side could be seductive for a Jedi. Vader knew that.

If it were so, he would have to take steps to eliminate Ferus Olin here, now. He couldn't allow Ferus Olin to flourish in the Empire. It wasn't ambition talking — Vader left ambition to fools like the captain of the battalion here — it was efficiency. He couldn't do his job if Olin were around, trying to replace him. It would just be tiresome. And annoying.

He activated the comlink to access the security guard at the main entrance of the Imperial headquarters. They'd taken over a bloc of government offices near the Hall of Ministers. "Has Ferus Olin returned?" he asked.

"Just a few minutes ago, Lord Vader."

"Send him to me."

Ferus appeared in less than a minute. Vader was surprised he didn't make him wait, just to show him that he could. But then again, Ferus didn't play those tiresome games that Bog Divinian relished.

"You wanted to see me, chief?"

Vader despised his flippancy. So unlike the way he'd been when they'd been Padawans together. One day Olin would find himself at the end of a lightsaber. Vader was looking forward to that moment.

"I want a report on the resistance."

Ferus frowned. "I guess you forgot — I don't report to you. It's okay, I know you've got a lot on your mind — all that resistance to crush. If that's all, I'll —"

"I am not interested in whatever the Emperor asked you to do. Give me the report."

Ferus lounged against the wall and crossed his arms. "You know that you're the big mystery among the Emperor's staff. Everyone wants to know who you are. Where you came from. How did you get involved with the Emperor? One day you weren't there. The next day you were."

Vader found it extremely vexing that Ferus wasn't afraid of him. He was used to feeling fear from those who were in his presence. Once, he had felt it from Ferus Olin. Olin had tumbled out from his hiding place in the Temple, looked up at Vader, and he'd almost laughed at the fear coming off him in waves. Olin had taken off like a frightened womp rat. Vader could have — *should* have — killed him then. But he'd let him go. He was more interested in embarrassing Malorum, the Inquisitor, than killing Olin. Let Malorum try to handle the intruder. He hadn't expected that with all those prowler droids and stormtroopers at his disposal, Malorum would be incompetent enough to fail.

Now Ferus Olin had the protection of the Emperor. He couldn't touch him. Yet.

Extremely trying.

He could so easily use the dark side of the Force, send Ferus's body flying through the air and slam it hard against the wall. Watch Olin break. But he couldn't. Palpatine had told him to keep his hands off.

"Not sharing today? Oh well. Maybe when we get to know each other a little better."

"I know you," Darth Vader said.

He said the words contemptuously, but Ferus picked up something behind his tone.

"You know me?"

Vader never second-guessed himself now. He so rarely made a mistake. He had reacted to the Ferus Olin he'd known. The obtuse, thick-headed, pompous Padawan. He had to remind himself that Olin must have changed. Ferus was quicker now, smarter.

Vader turned away. "I know what you are. I know what you want. You are transparent. Go."

He was surprised when Ferus didn't come back with a quip. He just went away.

I know you.

Why did those words freeze him in his tracks?

Ferus thought back on the way Vader had spoken. There was no special emphasis in his tone; it was the same deep, expressionless disembodied voice that issued from a breath mask.

Or was it? What was it that he'd caught? An emotion, a feeling, a taunt?

Something.

And whatever it was, it had struck the same chord in Ferus.

I know you.

He knew Vader, too.

He stopped in the hallway, stockstill with the shock of it. It washed over him, the possibility — and along with that, the searing knowledge of his own stupidity.

He had assumed Vader had sprung up from nowhere because Palpatine had wanted it that way. He had assumed that Vader had been like Darth Maul, an apprentice trained and kept concealed until he was needed.

He had never considered the possibility that Vader hadn't been concealed.

That Vader had, instead, been *turned.*

That Vader could be — incredibly, tragically, *unbelievably* — a former Jedi.

I know you.

Could it be? Ferus turned and looked back at Vader's closed door. His eyes burned. He had known so many Jedi, crossed paths with so many. Hundreds. And he was known to many. He had been Siri Tachi's apprentice, and all Jedi knew Siri Tachi.

He stared at the closed door, wondering at the presence behind it.

Who are you?

CHAPTER NINE

Trever used his liquid cable as a lifeline. He made it to the top of the crystal formation — barely. What he wouldn't give for a little Force ability, a little boost to his jumps. Because at this rate, he wasn't getting away from these guys, and the chase had been going on for far too long.

At least they aren't shooting at me.

Suddenly, a large hunk of crystal next to him fused into white heat and disappeared.

Uh, scratch that.

Trever ducked and jumped onto the next formation. He had about three more jumps until he ran out of formations and into thin air. Now the crystals he'd admired from the air turned into sharp needle-like edges that scraped his palms and knees and made it impossible for him to get firm footing.

Far below he saw the mystery speeder close to the crystal forest floor, zigzagging through formations while the Imperial speeder tried to keep up. As he watched, the Imperial speeder lost control of a tight turn and slammed into a rough crystal mountain. The speeder skidded along the ground, spun around, and came to a stop.

Trever leaped to the next formation, avoiding the blaster fire that pinged and blasted through the branch where he'd been standing just a moment before.

The other Imperial speeder made a tight turn and came back at him. He leaped again.

He was now officially out of room. He could use his liquid cable again, but there was nowhere to go.

Then he saw the mystery speeder zoom upward. It maneuvered directly below him. The cockpit canopy slid back.

It was a very long drop.

He leaped.

He landed awkwardly, one leg out of the speeder, but the pilot made a hard starboard turn with one hand and yanked him inside with the other, stabbed at the canopy control, and went into a screeching dive, all while Trever was trying to catch his breath.

"Try to hang on." The voice came from inside the helmet. He couldn't see the driver's face. The fingers on the controls were delicate and soft-looking, but within ten seconds Trever realized he was in the hands of an amazing pilot.

The speeder was pushed to maximum as they screamed around formations, squeezed through branchlike forms, zoomed up and back down into canyons. It was like being in one of the Podraces Ferus had told him about, the highly illegal ones that were held on Outer Rim planets.

They lost the pursuing Imperial airspeeder. The pilot slowed down, and Trever told his tripping heart to slow down, too.

"That was one galactic ride," he said, nearly out of breath.

The pilot headed into a deep, narrow canyon and snaked the vehicle around the trunk formations of crystals. Trever saw a sleek ship with a red body and a chromium hull pulled up under an overhang. They stopped there.

He got out, his legs still shaky. The pilot leaped off the speeder and removed the helmet, shaking out shoulder-length dark hair. She was a petite human woman of middle years, with piercing green eyes that matched the crystals around them.

"You're Flame, aren't you?" Trever asked.

"Who wants to know?"

"Your contact," Trever said. "Toma sent me."

Her gaze ticked up and down, from his boots to the top of his head. "Aren't you a little young?"

Annoyed, Trever ignored the comment. "I'm

Trever Flume. I started in the resistance on Bellassa."

She popped a water canister and took a swallow, tossing another one to him. "How'd you hook up with Toma?"

"We share the same hideout. I've got an Imperial death mark on my head." Trever tried not to sound like he was boasting, just stating a fact. He wanted this woman to know that he was someone to be reckoned with. "I've been traveling with Ferus Olin."

She looked interested for the first time. "I've been trying to find Ferus Olin. He was a hero of the resistance on Bellassa. Then he disappeared."

"Toma said you're trying to network the resistance movements in the Core Worlds."

"It's a start. We're not going to get anywhere if we're not organized." Flame sat astride a crystal formation that formed a sort of bench. "I've learned one thing in my life — great wealth makes things happen. If we can fund resistance movements through one central organization, we can make progress. All it takes is wealth. Wealth creates opportunity. Simple."

"Toma said you were one of the wealthiest citizens on Acherin."

She smiled. "I was loaded. Now I've got quite a bit stashed here and there, and I'm looking for more investors. It's not only freedom fighters who hate the Empire. There are some very rich businesspeople who fear their businesses being taken over. You can't sell goods in a galaxy ruled by fear."

"So are you in this for justice, or so you can create more wealth for yourself and your friends?" Trever asked.

"What's the matter with both? I'm a realist, not a dreamer. Most beings aren't idealists. Most want to know what's in it for them."

"You're speaking my language," Trever said admiringly.

"So, can you hook me up with Ferus Olin?"

"That's why I'm here. Toma thought we might be able to help each other."

She tossed the empty water canister into the speeder. "What's his deal? What's he trying to do?"

Trever wasn't about to spill the beans on the secret Jedi base. "Since I've been with him, he's been basically trying to escape from Imperial jails," he said. "You'll have to ask him that question."

"I have another mission here," Flame said. "I've got an idea that can help the resistance. What makes Samaria unique? And I don't mean this place," she said, waving a hand at the crystal formations around her. "Personal droids. Everyone has them — including the Imperial advisor. They gave him one to thank him for saving the city."

"He didn't save the city," Trever said. "He just took the credit."

"Doesn't matter. If he's got a personal droid, that means it's tracked his every move for the past two days. Listened in on every conversation. If we could get our hands on that droid. . . ."

"We might learn something."

"And it will be a way to show the resistance that I mean business. Stealing it won't be easy, though."

Trever grinned. "It will be for me."

CHAPTER TEN

Ferus was put through to the Emperor immediately. The hologram floated in front of him, full-size. Palpatine's hood was drawn over his head, and Ferus could only see a trace of the yellowish skin, the slash of a mouth.

"I have located the resistance and delivered your message."

"Excellent."

"They will consider your offer."

"Will they accept?"

Ferus was expecting this question. He thought the chance was zero, but he had to keep Palpatine happy and Vader away. "I think there is a slim chance," he said. "They are disheartened because the majority of Samarians don't support resistance. So they feel isolated. I don't get the sense that there are very many of them. They don't trust me, of course."

"Continue to monitor the situation. Did you gain

any information that would be helpful to Lord Vader?"

"Just a drop. The used speeder stand on Telos Street. But I'm sure they'll change it now. I haven't told him about it — my orders were to report to you first."

"I will inform him. You have done well, Ferus Olin."

"Lord Vader isn't happy that I'm reporting to you," Ferus added. He was hoping to probe Palpatine a bit.

"That is not your concern."

"It makes it hard to work together. Perhaps if I knew more about him . . ."

He saw Palpatine pause. He'd interested him. "So, you are becoming curious about Lord Vader."

"Everyone is curious about Lord Vader."

"He prefers mystery. It is helpful. You have something else. Uniqueness. You were trained in the Force, and you rejected it. All the Jedi have been eliminated, but the Force remains. You could use it again."

"I'm a little rusty," Ferus said. Palpatine thought he was corruptible.

"You managed to find a lightsaber."

"Lots of weapons around for sale after the Clone Wars. I managed to get my hands on one. It's a dangerous galaxy out there."

"You could have more power than any officer. More power," Palpatine rasped, "than even Lord Vader himself."

Here it was. The beginning.

"I'm not interested in power," Ferus said.

"Everyone is interested in power," Palpatine said. "But not everyone has the vision to see what *real* power can accomplish."

Ferus rested his hand on the hilt of his lightsaber. The Jedi hadn't been about power. They'd used the Force to bring justice to the galaxy. But in truth the Force gave them great power, and many Padawans wrestled with the concept of it. When to use it, when to retreat, when to advance, when to demolish an enemy, and when to let them go. It was a constant struggle. And what every Padawan could not admit, even to each other, at night on their sleep couches, for even a whisper might bring the dark side too close — power felt good.

Ferus had fought against that feeling, had denied it existed, had thought he'd conquered it . . . but had he really?

He had brought up the topic with Siri — because Siri was the kind of Master you could talk to about anything. One of the countless things he missed about her was how nothing he could ask could possibly shock or disappoint her.

They were together on one of the terraces of

the Temple. Siri had her booted feet propped up on a bench and was lying on the ground, her eyes closed. Ferus sat cross-legged (stiff as always, he thought now) by her side. It had been raining on Coruscant for weeks, and as soon as the sun appeared, she'd dragged him outside.

"For a lesson?" he had asked.

"For fun," she'd answered.

He had waited, gathering his courage. Only when he was sure she was completely relaxed did he bring up the subject. Maybe he was hoping she was asleep, and he wouldn't have to bring it up at all.

"Master, I've been thinking about something," he said. "I feel myself growing stronger in the Force. On this last mission . . . when we fought . . . I was . . . happy."

She opened one eye and looked at him. "Do you mean, when we fought side by side on Meldazar together, you felt pleasure in how you could move, could bring down your enemy with one stroke?"

"Yes." Ferus felt ashamed. "Is that wrong?"

"Well." She raised herself on her elbows. Sunlight picked out bright individual strands in her blond hair, which she'd recently cropped even shorter than usual.

"Yes," she said. "It is wrong to attach emotion

in a battle. It's wrong to feel pleasure when an enemy falls. A Jedi should feel regret — regret that a life has been taken, regret that a physical battle had to be fought at all. But the Force gives us great gifts, Ferus. It isn't wrong to take pleasure in your own gifts. To take pleasure in your mastery of skill. It's a struggle for every Jedi to attain balance, sometimes even for Jedi Masters. Look at Mace Windu. His style is Form VII. What do you know about Form VII?"

"That only the best fighters can control it."

"Exactly. It can bring you close to the dark side, to what the Sith focus on. But Mace Windu can control it. My point is that even Mace Windu must acknowledge this danger, of the pleasure in power. That's the only way he can dismiss it. In other words, my perpetually worried Padawan" — Ferus remembered her smile, the rare smile that was gentle, not mischievous or mocking — *"the fact that you ask the question guards you against the dangers of it."*

It had been a typical Jedi response. If you are aware of a problem, you take the first step toward eliminating it. Helpful at the time, but that was when he had a Temple to go to, Jedi Masters around him. All that careful study, all those simple and profound rules of the order — they had answered his every doubt.

Was leaving the Jedi a relief in a way because he never had to think about that again?

Why was he thinking about it now?

The memory and the questions had taken place in a mere flash of a moment, but Ferus was suddenly afraid. Afraid that too much time had passed between Palpatine's statement and his own response. Afraid that Palpatine had known, somehow, unerringly, exactly what he'd been thinking.

"This is an interesting conversation, but I have some duties to take care of," Ferus said, swallowing. His mouth was dry.

"Of course," the Emperor said.

The hologram disappeared. Ferus felt the light-saber hilt under his fingers. He ran his fingertips over the worn grooves in the carving. He thought of Garen Muln, the great Jedi Master who had given it to him. With that gift came responsibility, and also a connection to the way things used to be when he had a whole Jedi order to lean on. Before he was alone.

Give me your certainty, Garen, he thought. *Give me your courage.*

CHAPTER ELEVEN

Exercise was important. Bog got off the vibro-tonic all-muscle trainer and padded off to the shower. He shipped the all-muscle trainer from post to post because he knew the importance of fitness. It cleared his head. He didn't trust a being who didn't take care of him- or herself. He was never too busy for his daily routine. Excess flesh disgusted him. He didn't want to turn into a Hutt.

His comlink buzzed. His assistant's voice came through. "Sano Sauro trying to reach you."

"Tell him I'll contact him shortly."

"He won't like that."

"No," Bog said, grabbing a towel, "he won't."

Sano Sauro. He'd been helpful. Everyone thought he was the brains behind Bog. It was true that Sauro had been instrumental in plotting the moves to get Bog in a position of influence, but Bog was tired of Sauro thinking he was in control. And now that

Sauro's big idea, the *True Justice* ship that tried political prisoners in space, had been hijacked, he'd been censured by the Emperor. A little distance would be a good idea right about now, until Bog figured out if Sauro was out of the loop permanently or not.

In the meantime, let him sweat.

The forty-five minutes of training had focused Bog's mind, made it sharp. All the steps he had taken were paying off. The Emperor himself had come to Sath, and Bog didn't think he was exaggerating to say that it had just a bit to do with him. He was making his mark.

Nobody had ever believed in him. Not his father, not his wife. But he'd always believed in his destiny.

At the thought of Astri, Bog frowned involuntarily. He'd gotten over the fact that his wife didn't love him anymore, long ago. He hadn't expected love. He'd expected a partnership. He was a politician; it helped to have a pretty wife. She never understood her role. Well, it was his own fault for picking a cook in a greasy diner as a wife. His head had been turned by her curls and her smiles. Her closeness to the Jedi hadn't hurt at the time, either.

Now she was gone. Disappeared. It didn't look right that he didn't have contact with his own son. He'd find Lune one day. When he was ruler of Samaria he would have much more muscle. And he wouldn't need a vibrotonic all-muscle trainer to exercise it, either! Pleased at his joke and at the results of his workout, Bog stepped into the shower.

The vote of no-confidence would be a lock. He'd made sure of that. But a little insurance might not be a bad idea. Something to boost him even more with the population so that when he took over, the transition would be smooth.

Becoming ruler of Samaria was just the first step. Why couldn't he control the whole Lemurtoo system, and move on from there?

This was his moment. He didn't need Sauro's advice. He didn't need anyone's. He was ready to strike out on his own. Take the big chance.

He slipped into his tunic and picked up his com-link as it signaled again.

"Sano Sauro is waiting," his assistant said.

"Tell him I'm busy," Bog said. He smiled, thinking of how that would infuriate Sauro. Let him steam.

Bog placed his personal droid on his shoulder. What a useful little device it was turning out to be.

Sauro had taught Bog well. To control a population, one must create an enemy, something for them to be afraid of. Then save them from it. It was as simple as that.

CHAPTER TWELVE

For now, Ferus pushed the thought of who Vader might be to the back of his mind. It would be impossible to figure it out. Unless Vader made some kind of verbal slip or Ferus managed to stumble over new information, he wouldn't be able to discover it. He might never know.

What was he still doing here, anyway? Although he kept his eyes open, he hadn't learned very much about the Empire. Ferus had contacted the resistance, but he still wasn't sure how he could help them.

There were times that he felt he was doing absolutely the right thing for absolutely the right reasons. This was not one of those times.

He had been in the resistance on Bellassa, but he'd always been a reluctant hero. He'd fought briefly in the Clone Wars, but he hadn't been a great general like Obi-Wan. He hadn't adapted well to the army at all. He had fought side by side with Roan, but he hadn't been like the others, who'd joined the army for adventure. He'd seen adventure as a Jedi. He'd seen death and destruction and greed. He had no illusions about how thrilling great battles were. Great battles were hard and bloody and you never got the smell of it off you.

Maybe he wasn't that great at being a double agent, either. He had hoped to learn more about the Empire's plans. He'd hoped that getting close to Palpatine and Vader would afford him the opportunity to discover if any Jedi were known to be alive, or held prisoner. But he could see that although it appeared he had the confidence of Palpatine, he wasn't really given access to anything that might help. He could observe all he wanted, but what he was able to observe was carefully controlled. Vader, he was sure, controlled it.

Would they ever let him in?

The city of Sath was running smoothly; there were no protests or fears that the Empire would take over, but Ferus felt uneasy. There was no battalion here, and though he'd kept his eyes and ears open he'd found no evidence that they were around. If Bog lost the vote, Vader would need muscle.

What he still hadn't figured out was why Palpatine himself had turned his attention here, and why his enforcer, Vader, was here, too. Was he missing something?

He just wanted to go back to the secret base and forget about Samaria, but something inside wouldn't let him. He hadn't had a chance to talk to Roan, to see what he'd been up to on Bellassa. He wanted to steal time, just a few days, to spend with him. He wanted to make sure the base was thriving, that Raina and Toma had what they needed. He wanted to enlist Clive to help them. There were things to do.

Ferus moved through the city streets of Sath. He stopped at the Twilight Fountains and paused to watch the colored spray change from aquamarine to gold to deep orange to navy blue and back again. He felt sadness wash over him but couldn't determine the cause. On Somaria, he felt something sucking at his footsteps, draining him. It wasn't the plight of the planet. Was it the fact that he couldn't see his path clearly? He kept going, one step at a time, and now he found himself shoulder to shoulder with Vader and Palpatine. He was learning nothing except that he had a powerful impulse to flee.

The possibility of Vader being a fallen Jedi chilled him. How had it happened? How had he been corrupted? What terrible seduction drew him in?

"Ferus. Follow me."

The words were low, spoken by someone behind

his back. He recognized Nek's soft tone. He began to move along the fountain, not turning to glimpse her until he felt it was clear. Then he leisurely made his way through the crowds out enjoying the artificially cooled air. He followed her reddish curls and weaved his way to her as she stopped near a wall. She put her hands on the top and hauled herself up, then sat, legs kicking, a few meters away from others who had done the same.

Ferus pulled himself up beside her. He could see immediately why she'd chosen this spot to perch. The entire plaza was visible from here. Behind them was another wall. Another short jump would lead them to an upper walkway with access to several airbus routes and main thoroughfares. It would be relatively easy to lose a tail if they spotted one.

Still kicking her feet casually against the wall, Nek spoke in a worried voice. "We've got trouble. Maybe."

"Tell me."

"We've been monitoring some of Bog's activities through his PD. We've got evidence of bribery."

"That's good."

"There's something else . . . the personal droid has been linked up with two Roshan prowler droids."

"Aren't they illegal on Samaria?"

"Yes. He must have smuggled them in."

"Why would he do that?"

"Maybe he's going to do something and blame it on the Roshans. That's what we fear."

"What do you think it will be?"

"I don't know. But we were wondering . . ."

". . . if I could go check it out. Do you know where he is now?"

Nek nodded. "We have him in the government district — the diplomatic wing of the Residence Tower. He's meeting with the Roshan delegation."

"This can't be good," Ferus said. "I'll be in touch."

Ferus leaped to the next wall, then ran lightly down the walkway. He hailed an air taxi and gave the driver the address. He handed over a wad of credits. "If you get me there in less than five minutes, you'll get more."

The driver looked at the credits in her hand. "I'll get you there before you can blink, with these."

The air taxi moved quickly through the traffic, weaving in and out of lanes and accomplishing a few highly illegal maneuvers. The driver proudly pulled up in front of the Residence Tower in four minutes flat. Ferus pressed another wad of credits in her hand and jumped out.

He waved his Imperial security tag at the sensor and the light blinked green. Ferus hopped aboard the turbolift. Being a double agent occasionally had its advantages. At least he didn't have to waste time breaking in.

He was whisked up to the two hundredth floor, a central lobby for the block of floors where visiting diplomats were housed during their stays in Sath. He stepped out into a luxurious space. Ten different hallways spun out from the center. Ferus paused. He reached out for the Force. He picked up the Living Force around him. After only a moment he turned and sprinted down one of the hallways.

He paused in front of a transparisteel door. Outside was a combination landing platform and meeting room. The meeting room was encased in the same climate-controlled bubble that dotted many of the outdoor spaces in Sath. Bog Divinian sat in an informal grouping with the Roshan delegation. The usual empty smile was on Bog's face, and Ferus watched as he gestured around toward the city surrounding them.

Nothing had happened . . . yet.

Bog's personal aide, a slender young woman named Nancer, stood nearby. Ferus noted that Bog's airspeeder was outside on the landing platform. Two Imperial airspeeders were parked nearby, each with two stormtroopers inside. Bodyguards for Bog, Ferus imagined.

Ferus accessed the door and slipped into the

room. Nancer looked over at him but turned her attention back to Bog. She knew Ferus as a favorite of Palpatine's and would not interfere with him.

"So you see, even though I oppose the trade agreement, I don't oppose an alliance with Rosha, should I be elected," Bog was saying.

"Advisor Divinian, let us be frank," the senior Roshan diplomat said. Ferus remembered his name — Robbyn Sark. "You have spread misinformation about us among the people of Sath. Now they distrust our motives."

Bog waved his hands in the air as though he were swatting an insect. "Whether or not you had anything to do with sabotage of the Platform-7 computer —"

"No." Ferus admired Robbyn Sark's tone. The Roshan did not raise his voice, but the authority it carried had the power to silence even Bog Divinian. "We had nothing to do with the sabotage, and you know it. We are alone here, Advisor Divinian. Let's speak with honesty."

"Of course," Bog said blandly. "I'm a straight shooter. Always have been."

"You are opposing the trade agreement for your own reasons. They have nothing to do with the well-being of the two planets. Let's discuss how we could work together. You said you wanted to find a compromise."

"That's why I'm here," Bog said. "Let's find some common ground. I have a proposition for you. My speeder is outside. Come with me for a short trip around Sath. I have some things to show you. We can discuss the current situation in privacy."

Bog looked around the meeting room and leaned forward. "You can never trust meeting rooms where diplomats stay," he whispered. "We can speak freely in my speeder."

Robbyn Sark glanced at the four other Roshans. A signal passed between them. Their delicate antennae, which looked more like tiny hairs, waved softly.

"All right," Robbyn Sark agreed.

Ferus followed, still unsure of what Bog was up to. He trailed after the others as they walked out onto the landing platform. Like all the platforms on Sath, it was regulated with cool air from the floor and overhang, and a fine mist also served to freshen the air.

Still, before them the buildings of Sath seemed to shiver in the heat, their outlines wavy and indistinct. The sun was low in the sky, at exactly an angle to bounce off the thousands of windows and the thin metallic skins of the buildings. It dazzled the eye and disoriented him. It took Ferus a moment to realize that the glint in the air above was not a reflection, but a moving airspeeder, coming at them at a direct angle and not slowing down to land. At the same time, something else caught his attention — at first he thought it was debris in the air. The specks were moving erratically, as if caught by a breeze. But there was no breeze.

Their droids are among the smallest in the galaxy with the most sophisticated systems.

Roshan droids.

Bog didn't seem to notice any of it. He fiddled with the PD on his shoulder as he gestured grandly at his luxurious airspeeder, saying something to Robbyn Sark that Ferus didn't hear.

"Watch out!" Ferus shouted, but it was too late. The silver airspeeder came in low and fast. Then to Ferus's astonishment the engines stopped dead. He saw a slight hooded figure in black lying flat on the hull. A liquid cable line snaked down and wrapped around Bog's personal droid. It was yanked upward.

Ferus saw Bog's frightened face as he dropped to the ground. The engines screamed back to maximum. Ferus was already moving, racing to the nearest airspeeder on the platform.

In the meantime, the stormtroopers had finally reacted and were blasting away at the fleeing airspeeder. Bog covered his head. The two Roshan droids turned and gave chase.

Ferus made the quick calculations even as he pushed the controls of the speeder. Someone had stolen Bog's personal droid, and it wasn't the resistance. They had no reason to. They had every reason for Bog to retain the droid. They knew what was on it. The proof of Bog's bribes were embedded in its programming. Ferus had to get the droid back.

The silver airspeeder headed straight for the thickly clustered tall buildings of Sath. The stormtroopers behind him didn't seem to mind if Ferus got caught in the middle. Swerving to avoid the fire behind him, Ferus moved to an upper traffic lane. With any luck the thief would notice only the stormtroopers in pursuit, not him.

He pushed his speed, trying to keep the silver speeder in sight below him but not attract attention. He saw the Roshan droids tracking, occasionally sending a thin beam of energy blasting toward the silver speeder that seemed so accurate Ferus was always surprised when it missed.

Screaming through the Sathan skies, Ferus called on the Force to help him maneuver. He pulled up just in time to avoid smashing into an airbus. The glare of the flashing reflections, the buzzing of the Roshan droids, and the traffic around and below him kept him busy.

Whoever was piloting the speeder sure knew how to fly. Ferus soared high above the speeder, tracking it through the space lanes. One droid sent an arc of blaster fire toward it, but the speeder flipped over, flew upside down, and spiraled into an opening in the traffic above. Ferus had to admire the pilot's skill.

Who was it? If it wasn't the resistance, who could it be?

CHAPTER THIRTEEN

"I think you can slow down," Trever said through clenched teeth. "The stormtroopers are falling behind."

"You don't slow down until you're home free," Flame said. "They aren't giving up. They're just trying to make me think they're giving up. I'd better drop you somewhere with the droid. Then we can meet up later. You can lose the speeders a lot easier on foot."

"Drop me?" Trever asked as Flame flipped the craft to one side to squeeze in between two buildings. "I don't like the sound of that."

"Don't worry." Flame laughed. "I'll get you down in one piece." She shot him an admiring glance. "I like your style, kid. You swiped that droid like a pro."

"I *am* a pro," Trever said. "I mean, I might have done a bit of, uh, unauthorized lifting of goods on

Bellassa." He shrank back as Flame zoomed into a tunnel, hugging the top of it to keep in the shadows. Trever felt as though the top of his head was going to slam against the wall of the tunnel.

"Funny how skills like that come in handy in the resistance," Flame said. As soon as they shot out of the tunnel, she flipped over and quickly descended three space lanes. "I got most of my piloting skills from avoiding air traffic tickets."

Trever watched as she flew and scanned the buildings around at the same time. He glanced behind. The droids were still tailing them, but he couldn't see the stormtroopers now.

"This is our chance," she murmured. "The droids will follow me, most likely. I'm going to drop down into one of the courtyards. You're going to have to jump. Then start running. I'll contact you on your comlink when I think it's safe."

"All right." Trever crouched on his seat, Bog's droid on his shoulder.

The airspeeder dropped so quickly Trever felt sure he'd left his stomach up in the space lane. But there was no time to get dizzy. The ground loomed toward him. The cockpit canopy rolled back, and the wind blew in his face. He snapped his helmet cover down.

"If someone follows you, shoot," Flame said, tossing him a blaster. "Now jump!"

Ferus flew, taking chance after chance. With the help of the Force, he was finding holes in traffic to slip through that didn't exist fractions of a second before. The speeder below had lost the stormtroopers, but for how long?

In answer, he saw the stormtroopers suddenly appear, bursting out of a tunnel that the speeder had disappeared into. Suddenly the silver speeder below reversed direction and went into a dive. The stormtrooper airspeeders overshot it, tried to reverse, and made an awkward spinning turn that nearly sent one into an airbus while the other clipped a building. A tremendous air traffic snarl instantly locked everyone in place.

Ferus merely reversed his engines and went backward, cursing as he looked over his shoulder and tried to gauge distances between vehicles and swerving from one space lane to another. He saw the silver speeder drop into a courtyard while the droids streaked past, just missing the speeder's fast descent.

Ferus hit a hard right and hovered over a landing platform twenty stories up, monitoring the last of the silver speeder's descent. Someone tumbled out and the speeder zoomed off while the thief disappeared belowground into some sort of parking facility. Ferus parked his own vehicle and leaped out in one smooth movement, then Force-jumped twenty stories to the courtyard below.

He couldn't tell if the thief was a man or woman; he just knew whoever it was was slight and could run fast. He'd barely gotten a glimpse before the thief disappeared into the parking hangar.

He heard running footsteps on the permacrete and took off, snaking through parked speeders, ready to activate his lightsaber. He leaped over one speeder, and blasterfire streaked toward him. He lifted his lightsaber to deflect it back but stopped.

"Ferus! Don't!"

In a split second of incredible timing, Ferus managed to halt his movement and somersault away from the energy blasts. He leaped over the last speeder and onto the ground.

"Trever?"

Trever slowly rose, his head peeking over a cockpit canopy. "You know, you're pretty good with that thing. A guy could get killed."

"What are you doing?" Ferus asked furiously. His hands were shaking. He had come close to deflecting fire back at Trever. He pushed the image of the boy lying on the ground, lifeless, out of his mind. *Acknowledge the mistake, and move on.*

Or, as Siri used to say, *There's always time to kick yourself later.*

He sprang forward and yanked on Trever's arm,

pulling him into the relative safety of the shadows near the great pillars that held up the roof of the hangar.

"I'm helping the resistance," Trever said, shaking off Ferus's hand.

"I don't think so. Who was driving that speeder?"

"Flame. Toma was in contact with her."

"Who's Flame?" Ferus grabbed the droid. "Actually, I don't have time for this now — I have to get this back to Bog."

"You're going to take it *back?* Do you have any idea how hard it was to get it?"

"What are you doing here, anyway?"

"Helping you."

"I've got news for you." Ferus tucked the droid under his arm. "You're not helping."

"Watch out!" Suddenly, Trever slammed into Ferus, sending him flying. At the same time, Ferus saw the droids darting through the air, straight for him.

CHAPTER FOURTEEN

Ferus pushed Trever under a heavy speeder and whirled up, clutching Bog's droid in one hand and his lightsaber in the other. The droids followed.

Why him and not Trever? He'd assumed they'd locked on Trever earlier. Their beaming accuracy had been aimed at the fleeing speeder. He'd been sure that they'd hit several times . . .

Wait a second.

Ferus backed up, leaping up on the roof of a speeder. Red beams of blaster energy shot out toward him. Instead of deflecting them, he stood motionless.

"Ferus!" Trever screamed.

The beams passed over him harmlessly. Just as he'd suspected.

Ferus put Bog's droid on the top of the speeder and jumped down. The droids circled and came back.

This time when they approached, he leaped up and caught both of them easily, one in each hand.

"Wow," Trever said.

Ferus sat, turning the droids over in his hands. He checked the weapons system displays. Trever approached curiously. "What are you doing?"

"That blaster fire was benign. There was no charge. I'm just wondering why."

"We got lucky?"

"And they were locked onto Bog's personal droid." Ferus thought back to the moment on the landing platform when Trever had swiped Bog's droid. The Roshan droids had *already* been moving toward it. They'd been locked on to Bog's droid. For what? A demonstration?

Ferus stood, tucking the two Roshan droids into his pocket. "Come on. We've got to get back."

A disgruntled Trever followed him without a word. He quickly found the turbolift to the landing platform above. Ferus climbed into the pilot seat and indicated a cargo space in the back. "You're going to have to hide in there." As Trever began to protest, Ferus cut him off. "Just do it. And don't say a word. I'll explain later."

He powered up the engines and rose into the traffic lanes. He saw patrolling airspeeders with stormtroopers, and some now on swoop bikes, flooding the space lanes, looking for the silver craft. Ferus avoided them and entered a stream of traffic back toward the Residence Tower. The whole adventure had taken less than ten minutes.

He came in high, leaving Bog plenty of time to identify him. Stormtroopers ringed the platform, blaster rifles ready.

"Whoa. Maybe you'd better rethink this approach," Trever whispered, peeking out of the cargo compartment.

"Stay down! It's all right — they think I'm one of them, remember?"

As Ferus brought the vehicle down, he saw that Bog had retreated into the meeting room again. The Roshan delegation was gone. Bog was speaking to a short Sathan that Ferus recognized as the lead communications officer. A few other Sathans were in the room. Ferus tried to glimpse them through the glare of transparisteel. They looked like . . . reporters?

He got out, holding the droid. Bog saw him from inside. He said a few quick words to the others and came out, hurrying toward Ferus.

Ferus handed him the droid.

"You got it back." Bog's eyes narrowed. "Who took it?"

"Just a common street thief, looking for something to sell on the black market."

"Is the womp rat in custody? I'd like to fry him up for breakfast."

A squeak came from the speeder. Luckily, Bog didn't hear it.

"No," Ferus said. "He dropped the droid, I caught it, and came back here. I guess he realized it was a stupid idea."

"Did you have any trouble . . . getting back here?"

"No."

Was that a flash of relief on Bog's face? He perched the droid back on his shoulder. "I thought coming here to speak to the delegation would make a difference. Bridge the gap." He shook his head. "I never expected they'd have the nerve to try to assassinate me."

"What?"

Bog leaned in. "Those droids . . . in the air? We ran a security check on them during the attack. They were Roshan. There was blasterfire coming from them, straight at me. Luckily, I have good reflexes."

"The droids didn't shoot at you. That blasterfire was from the stormtroopers. They were aiming at the thief!"

Bog frowned at him. "You couldn't know that."

"I was standing only a few meters away," Ferus said. "The shots came from the stormtroopers. They were shooting at the speeder."

He had the Roshan droids in his pocket. But they would prove nothing. Handing them over now would just confirm their existence and give more credibility to Bog's lie.

But now Ferus understood. This was all a ploy for Bog to gain sympathy. Bog had done this himself. He had set up the situation. The Roshan droids had been programmed to fire at his droid. It was Trever's bad luck that he happened to steal Bog's droid at the same time. But Bog had turned the incident to his advantage. He would claim the thief was part of the Roshan plot.

Ferus was trapped. He couldn't expose Bog without exposing Trever.

Bog leaned in toward him, his eyes like slits. Ferus found himself looking into a gaze empty of intelligence but full of menace. Ferus wasn't intimidated, but he did see that if he interfered with what Bog was planning, the politician would not take it lightly.

"Since there is no way for you to have really seen it, I hope you keep your mistaken impressions to yourself," he said. "You think that because the Emperor has given you amnesty that he can't revoke that order at any time? The Emperor came to *my* planet, to *my* ceremony. Who do you think he's going to believe?"

"*Your* planet?" Ferus said. "Since when?"

"Just don't get in my way," Bog warned.

Ferus watched as Bog turned away, the droid still on his shoulder. He walked back into the meeting room while the reporters scrambled to get close.

He was about to spin the story for all of Samaria.

Ferus had a bad feeling. A very bad feeling.

Bog overestimated his own importance. He was just a tool to the Emperor.

So was Ferus.

Trapped.

This time, Ferus signed out the airspeeder, which was registered to the Residence Tower. Trever hid in the back until they were safely away. Ferus pulled up at the Twilight Fountains.

Trever hopped out, a disgruntled look on his face. "I can't believe you took the droid back. I went to a lot of trouble to steal it."

"It was a stupid idea. If you want to help the resistance, you don't just bumble your way in. You contact them first!"

"Flame thought they wouldn't take her seriously if she didn't pull of some kind of mission first —"

"Who's Flame?" Ferus interrupted.

"I told you, a contact of Toma's." The boy looked sulky now. "She had gravsleds full of wealth on Acherin — factories and businesses and all that —

but she had one problem. She said no to the Empire, so they kicked her off the planet. But she was able to get most of her wealth out before that. She put it all into this group she's forming called Moonstrike. She has this idea to fund all the resistance groups on planets in the Core. And she's putting her own wealth and her own safety on the line. Plus she's one awesome pilot. She's galactic."

"So Toma set up this meeting? He sent you?" Ferus knew Trever well by now. He saw the lie beginning to form on the boy's face. "Toma didn't send you. You came yourself."

"Well, they weren't about to consider me. But it was too dangerous for any of them. So I . . ."

"You . . ."

"Took the ship," Trever mumbled. "And came here."

"You left them without a ship?"

"So? They didn't have one before!"

"Where is the ship now?"

"In the Crystal Forest."

"All right. As soon as we finish here, I want you to get back there, get the ship, and go back to the base."

"Yessir, General Ferus-Wan, sir," Trever said. "Except for one thing. There's no more ship."

Ferus closed his eyes. "No more ship?"

"I sort of crashed it."

Ferus didn't want to believe it, but could. "Did anyone see you?"

"Just a couple of stormtroopers. But I got away in Flame's speeder. It was one incredible ride, let me tell you. And this idea of the central funding of resistance groups — she's got all these plans to mobilize, and find other investors . . . we've got to bring her to the resistance here so that they can join Moonstrike."

"I'm not taking her to the resistance."

"Why not?"

"Trever, she could be anyone."

"But Toma knows her!"

"What you told me was that she contacted Toma. He doesn't know if she's for real, either. I can't endanger the resistance by bringing a stranger to them."

"She's not a stranger!"

"I'll bring them her message, that's all." Ferus looked at Trever carefully. "Did you tell her about the secret base?"

"Of course not! I wouldn't do that — I'm not completely stupid. But I do think she could help. We need more supplies there. Toma and Raina have been having a hard time. She could fund the base, fund your search. This could be our chance to really build something, not just a base for a couple of Jedi."

Ferus shook his head through Trever's speech. "If the base is to succeed, it has to be small. And the fewer beings who know about it, the better. Even if Flame checks out, I don't want to link the base to a galaxy-wide resistance movement — not yet, anyway."

"But that's the only way we'll defeat the Empire."

"I know that. But moving prematurely could endanger all of us. I created the base in order to gather Jedi. Period. If we get too ambitious, we could risk everything. The base must remain a secret."

"You've got some weird wacky Jedi obsession, that's your problem," Trever grumbled. "They kicked you out, so now you have to prove that you're worthy or something."

"They didn't kick me out," Ferus said. "I left. And this search has nothing to do with me. It has to do with saving anything that might be left." Ferus struggled with his own annoyance at what the boy had said. "An alliance of resistance groups is necessary, I agree. But I am beginning to understand this: In the end, only the Force will defeat the Emperor."

Obi-Wan had tried to tell him that. He hadn't

been ready to listen. He thought of Obi-Wan now, in self-imposed exile on Tatooine. *The hardest thing to do,* Obi-Wan had said, *is to wait.*

What was Obi-Wan waiting for? Ferus had thought that it had to do with waiting in the abstract. Waiting for luck, waiting for chance, waiting for the galaxy to begin to rise up. Now he realized something: Obi-Wan was waiting for something specific. Ferus didn't know what. He wasn't meant to know. Obi-Wan couldn't tell him. But somehow, Obi-Wan had hope.

"Look, I've seen the Force work," Trever said. "I know it's full-moon amazing and all that. But it isn't *everything.* It's just a part of what can bring them down. You aren't giving Flame a chance."

"I will give her a chance," Ferus said. "But not with the base. I'll bring her message to the resistance."

"Take me with you."

"No. You know how a resistance works. A resistance can only operate if the fewest people possible know who is in the group."

"You don't trust me."

"Of course I trust you. But this is the best way, Trever. Now let me figure out how to get you another ship. You've got to get off-planet. There might be an Imperial crackdown on air traffic very soon. You're lucky you weren't blasted out of the sky."

"Is this what you were like as a Jedi Padawan? No wonder no one liked you," Trever burst out.

Ferus stopped short as Trever's words hit him in the face. He stood still for a moment as the meaning sank in.

As much as he wanted to control this, he couldn't. He had to stop underestimating Trever. He was treating him like a child, and he wasn't. Siri would have known that. Obi-Wan would have known that. Trever had been through so much. He'd done so much. He was capable of so much more.

"Yes," Ferus admitted. "You're right. That's what I was like." Then he sighed. "Okay, I'll contact the resistance. I'll tell them about you. This is a meeting place, right here. They'll find you. You'll be able to tell Flame's story your own way, and they can make the decision whether to meet with her. Fair enough?"

"Fair enough," Trever said, but his jaw was still set.

Ferus's comlink signaled. He looked at it. He was wanted back at Imperial headquarters. He hated to leave things like this with Trever.

"I have to go," he said.

"Oh, is the Emperor calling you?" Trever asked in a stinging tone. "Ready to do his bidding?"

"You know why I'm doing this," Ferus said.

Trever looked at him, his expression clouded with his disappointment. "Not really. I know this, though: If you get that close to evil, it can rub off on you."

Ferus walked away, toward the speeder. He had no answer to give Trever.

Because deep in his heart, he suspected that Trever was right.

CHAPTER FIFTEEN

Darth Vader wanted to avoid this particular discussion with his Master, but he could not. Palpatine appeared in hologram form, his hands tucked into the pockets of his robe.

"I received a report that there was an assassination attempt on Divinian's life," the Emperor began.

"Doubtful," Vader replied. "I have received contradictory reports. Divinian wants to be a hero and is blaming the Roshans."

"I am starting to be impressed by our Bog."

Vader's voice remained cold. "He wants to rule Samaria. He wants real power."

"His personal droid was retrieved by Ferus Olin."

"I have requested a full report from him," Vader said.

"Your stormtroopers went after the thief, but it was Ferus Olin who was successful."

This was exactly why he didn't want to have this talk.

Vader decided to change the subject. "Roshan droids were spotted as well. I think they were set off by Divinian."

"Interesting." The Emperor laughed softly to himself.

"With the assassination attempt, his support is greater than ever. Sathans will think Larker is a fool for trusting the Roshans."

"A good sign."

"My presence here is no longer required, then?"

"Wait and make sure Divinian is elected. I want an Imperial governor in every capital city."

"Divinian will be elected, just as you planned, my Master."

Palpatine continued, "In the meantime . . . Ferus Olin's power is growing. I sense great . . . uncertainty in him."

"Will he join us?"

Palpatine smiled. "He will become one of us."

The hologram of his Master faded. Darth Vader didn't move.

No. Not Ferus Olin.

It was time to get rid of him.

Olin was a reminder of his past. His past was dead. Olin must follow.

CHAPTER SIXTEEN

Ferus appeared in Darth Vader's office. "At your service."

"I have a job for you," Vader said.

"I take orders from the Emperor."

"The Emperor has commanded me. You can check with him if you like." Vader assumed that Ferus would decide not to. And even if he did, his Master had told him to help Bog Divinian before the vote. He could always claim that this was his intent.

"What's the job?"

"Find the thief who stole Bog Divinian's personal droid." Vader enjoyed the look of surprise on Ferus Olin's face.

"But the droid has been returned —"

"The thief was involved in the assassination attempt."

"There was no assassination attempt," Ferus said

impatiently. "Bog made it up to make himself look like a hero."

"All the more reason to find the thief. If someone appears who can denounce Divinian, it could influence the vote."

"I can't find him again — I didn't see much."

"I'm sure you will be able to. If you fail, I will institute mass arrests. A battalion orbiting Lemurtoo is awaiting my order to invade."

There. At last. Ferus Olin looked uneasy.

"I think this is a bad idea —"

"I am not interested in your opinion, Ferus Olin," Vader said.

Ferus turned and walked out.

Vader had threatened him and gained his cooperation.

A small victory. But tasty enough to savor.

Ferus stood in the hallway outside the door. He couldn't turn in Trever, of course. But he had no doubt that Vader would follow through on his threat. In the meantime, there were only a few hours before the no-confidence vote in the ministers' hall. It was time for the resistance to mobilize and expose Bog.

At the very least, it would serve as a distraction.

As he stood, his heartbeat quickened. Something was different. He listened carefully. Usually the sounds at headquarters were muffled and indistinct.

But he could hear voices and footsteps. It wasn't as though the place was coming alive . . . it was just more activity than usual.

He saw a nervous-looking junior officer heading down the hall. Ferus pretended to walk by him, then doubled back. The officer was speaking into a comlink.

Ferus kept well behind him, but accessed the Force. He screened out all the other noise and concentrated on that one voice.

"The troops are mobilized and ready for his order. Yes, sir. Garrison has been shifted to Order Thirty-Seven. Delegation is making plans to depart, but they are still quartered in the tower."

Thirty-seven. Ferus knew that directive from his time on Bellassa. It meant that mass arrests were planned.

Ferus reversed direction again and headed for the exit, his heart pounding. Vader had lied to him. He had already given an order to his battalion. They were standing by. But who was he targeting?

Ferus had little doubt the Roshan delegation would be first.

He found Dinko, Nek, and Firefolk talking to Trever and Flame at the cantina. Ferus took a seat at the table. He nodded at Flame. If the resistance had included her, he would have to as well.

"I've heard a lot about you," she told him.

"I've got news," he said. "The Imperial battalion is on alert."

"For what?" Dinko asked. "Invasion?"

"My guess is that they're in reserve in case Bog isn't elected. Anyone who protests will find themselves in an Imperial jail."

"It's happening," Nek said. "What we feared for so long."

"Is there anything we can do to stop this?" Flame asked.

Ferus frowned. "We're missing something. What does the Empire have against Rosha? Why do they want to stop the trade agreement? They're willing to invade a planet that isn't even hostile to them."

"We've had a rivalry with the Rosha, but lately we've realized that we can benefit each other," Dinko said. "Before Bog started spreading lies about Rosha, diplomacy was working."

Ferus took out the two Roshan droids and put them on the table. Firefolk leaned over with interest. "I've never actually seen these," he said. "It's illegal to import them." Firefolk began to tinker with one of the droids, snapping off its control panel. "I'm a systems designer. This is a whole new technology to learn."

Ferus leaned toward him. "Larker told me that the Roshans were experts in microtechnology."

Firefolk nodded, still examining the droid. "Part of our rivalry, of course, was based on fear. Fear that their droids could invade our systems." He let out a low whistle. "Would you look at this. A universal receiver microchip. And a remote sensory plug-in . . . with amazing range. I heard a rumor they'd developed this stuff, but . . ."

"What is it?"

"They can transfer information from any mainframe without a plug-in. This is an amazing delivery system. They can do it from distances, from the air." Firefolk took out his datapad and began to run tests on the droid. "It's got a direct system pathway to the photoreceptors and the movement sensors, so I'm guessing this is a way for the droid to read another droid's programming . . . so it can avoid collision, say, or duplication. All in less than a second. On a world with heavy droid use like Rosha, it would be a necessity. Their droids fly, ours just hover. So in less than a second, they can single out what they need to know — the other droid's path, for example, so they can make a countermove. I've seen versions of this, but this is way beyond. Technically, it's highly sophisticated."

"Wait a second," Ferus said. "You mean they read the other droid's programming and analyze it?"

Firefolk looked at his datapad, which was now interfaced with the droid. "They don't read it, they duplicate it, *transfer* it to their own system, analyze what they need, and then dump it."

"Couldn't they steal it, then?"

"I see where you're going with this," Firefolk said. "Not really. It has to be garbaged out. A droid this size doesn't have near the capacity to hold on to that much information. It can receive it, but it can only process a bit of it. If the droid kept all that information, it would overload and self-destruct."

Ferus felt an excitement rise up from his boots. "But here in Sath, you've pioneered the delivery of vast amounts of information from a BRT to a personal droid."

"Yes, it's loaded on from mainframes that we have at home, or at businesses we frequent. And we have what we call safeguard passageways to avoid overloading the droid," Dinko explained.

"What if the technology of both droids were put together?" Ferus asked. He turned to the others excitedly. "The Roshan droid has the ability to pull information from another droid. The Samarian droid has the ability to hook up to a vast BRT system. What if you built a super-droid that could grab enormous amounts of information without a plug-in? What if the droid could scramble the information and then send it all into a *second* droid?"

Firefolk sat still for a minute, thinking. "You mean pass random information from a BRT to another droid? It would have to be super fast. It's possible in theory . . . but that means that a vast amount of information would be passed back."

Dinko let out a breath. "If we married our BRT system software to their droid system software . . ."

Nek leaned forward. ". . . but used the hardware of our PDs . . . we target any droid and pass a flood of information to it. . . ."

". . . and the targeted droid would overload," Firefolk said.

Flame let out a breath. "Like a commander battle droid?"

"Or any Imperial droid?" Trever asked. "This is . . ."

"Unbelievable," Firefox murmured. "But . . . possible."

"And that is why," Ferus said, "the Emperor doesn't want a trade agreement between Samaria and Rosha. Because together you are a real danger to the Empire. If you could really do this, you could knock out their surveillance droids. Maybe even the stormtrooper communications systems. Everything they depend on for keeping the galaxy under their control."

"Just with our personal droids," Nek breathed. "Just by being able to transfer too much information."

"How do you like that," Trever said. "Buy a

cup of tea, annihilate an army. All in a droid's day's work!"

"And if you exported your system to other planets . . ." Ferus said.

"It's the key to a galaxy-wide resistance," Flame said. Her cheeks were flushed. "Moonstrike could fund it."

"Wait a second," Ferus said. "Remember, we're not the first to put this together. That's why they want to control Samaria. So they can move on to Rosha, too. Control both your worlds and stop any information exchange before it starts. I don't know whether Divinian is in on it or not — I'd doubt it. He's not high up enough and they don't value him . . . but he's played right into their plan. Now they'll arrest the Roshan delegation and imprison them. They can't let them get back to Rosha. They've had meetings with technicians here. Sooner or later they might figure it out, too."

Firefolk's hands were careful as he placed the droid back on the table. "What do we do now?"

"We bring this idea to the Roshan delegation," Ferus said. "And we've got to get them off-planet. The Empire is monitoring all departures, so getting them out will be tricky. They can't leave from Sath. And they can't use their own ship."

"The Crystal Forest. I can do it," Flame said. "I've got the ship. I'll get them home."

Ferus nodded. "In the meantime, the resistance has to influence the no-confidence vote. Bog must be exposed. Now is the time. The vote is scheduled to take place in less than an hour. I'll go with Flame and Trever and smuggle out the Roshans."

Dinko nodded. "Nek and Firefolk and I will head for the Hall of Ministers."

Dinko, Nek, and Firefolk hurried out of the cantina.

"I've only got one more problem," Ferus said.

"What?" Trever asked.

Ferus thought of Darth Vader and his ultimatum. He'd like to think that Vader would be too busy in a little while to care, but he knew in addition to being an evil mastermind, Vader was an awesome multi-tasker.

He looked at Trever. Affection washed over him, and he smiled at the boy's earnest expression underneath that thatch of blue hair. "You."

CHAPTER SEVENTEEN

Ferus didn't know what to expect when he, Flame, and Trever arrived at the Residence Tower. The landing platform on level two hundred was empty of stormtroopers. He parked the airspeeder and was able to enter the tower without a problem. Obviously the Empire's forces were not expecting a rescue attempt. Why should they? The Samarians were now convinced that the Roshans were their enemies.

Ferus walked out into the small lobby. There was a datascreen set into the wall by the central reception area. He keyed in the Roshan delegation and the screen flashed a room number ten stories above.

Ferus accessed the turbolift and they jumped on. They exited on the two hundred and tenth floor. Ferus silently moved toward the corner that would give him a vantage point into the hall. He quickly ducked back. The door to the Roshan suite was being patrolled by six Prowler 1000 droids and several dwarf spider droids.

He quickly explained the situation to Flame and Trever. "It won't be a problem," he said. "I can take them down. But they'll send a signal back, and reinforcements will be sent."

Flame patted her blaster. "We'll be ready."

Ferus turned to Trever. "Do you have any of your smoke grenades?"

"I happen to have a couple right here," Trever said, reaching into his utility belt.

"Save them for now. We'll need a way out of here. Okay, as soon as I take care of the droids, follow me."

Ferus activated his lightsaber. Flame's eyes grew wide.

"Did I mention he once trained to be a Jedi?" Trever asked.

Ferus charged into the hallway. The prowler droids immediately darted toward him like a flock of angry birds. He leaped up, slashing the first one into smoking bits, then reversed and took out two more. Meanwhile the spider droids sent blaster fire his way. He deflected it back to one, which burst into flame. He took out the other spider droid and casually sliced the last prowler in two with a backward swipe as he strode to the door.

He heard Flame's soft voice from down the hall. "No, Trever. You didn't mention it."

Ferus opened the door.

Robbyn Sark and the rest of the delegation stood in the middle of the room, blasters in their hands. All of them were pointed at him. Obviously they had heard the commotion in the hallway.

"We do not recognize your authority," Robbyn Sark said. "We will not subject ourselves to arrest."

"I'm not here to arrest you," Ferus said, deactivating his lightsaber and clipping it back to his belt. "I'm here to take you home."

Trever ran in. "We've got trouble. Stormtroopers entering the building and more spider droids. That didn't take long."

"We've got to get to the landing platform. We can't take the turbolift," Ferus said. "We'll take the stairs."

"There are no stairs," Robbyn Sark said.

"We'll have to chance the turbolift, then. Or . . ." Ferus strode to the windows. "We could launch a liquid cable, but we'll be spotted. They can pick us off if they have the range. And they do."

"There might be another way," Robbyn Sark said. "The utility lift. It's used for linens and room-service trays. It won't fit all of us at once, but it will hold a few of us at a time."

"Good idea." Ferus turned to Trever. "Set off some smoke grenades in all the turbolift banks. Fast."

"I'm on it." Trever took off.

Robbyn Sark led them to the utility turbolift. It was a small, squat lift where droids bundled laundry and delivered room-service trays. There was enough room for three at a time, if they crouched and squeezed.

"I'll go down with the first load," Ferus said. "Just in case there's trouble. Can you stay here and help the rest of the Roshans?" he asked Flame.

"I won't leave them," she promised.

Robbyn Sark and another delegation member entered, bending over and fitting their bodies into the space. Ferus followed, squeezing in next to them. He hit the sensor for the two-hundredth floor. As they descended, the first fire alarms began to ring. "Don't worry, it's just the smoke grenades," he told them. "They'll have to evacuate the building — or at least part of it. We can use that as cover for our escape."

"We'll have to get to our ship," Robbyn Sark said. "No doubt it will be heavily guarded."

"I've already found you a ride," Ferus said. "And I've seen her flying skills. She'll get you back to Rosha."

"Why are you doing this?" Robbyn Sark asked.

"I've got a long answer to that question," Ferus said.

The sound of explosives suddenly came to their ears. "I'll take the short version," Robbyn Sark said.

They reached the two-hundredth floor. Ferus emerged first, listening carefully. He sent the utility turbolift back up. There was the muted sound of activity, doors opening and closing, footsteps. The evacuation had begun. Smoke was out in the hall-way, but they covered their faces with their hoods and moved quickly.

He led the Roshans to the landing platform. As soon as they were outside, they took gulps of air. He quickly led them to the speeder and then real-ized his mistake — it was too small. Fortunately, larger transport was parked nearby, a luxury model with plenty of seating.

While they waited for the others, Ferus quickly told Robbyn Sark of what he and the resistance had come up with. Sark listened, his antennae waving softly.

"I don't know if it's possible," he said. "But if it is . . ."

The others came bursting through the doors. They quickly climbed into the luxury airspeeder. Having already overridden the security code, Ferus pushed the engines as the first stormtroopers burst out to guard the platform. A burst of blasterfire chased them into a space lane.

Quickly Ferus dipped down into a lower space lane and dived into an express tunnel. "I'm taking you to the Crystal Forest," he said.

As he flew, Ferus accessed the comm unit to contact Dinko and the others. Dinko's harried voice came through the cockpit speaker.

"It's over," he said. Even through the crackling transmission, Ferus picked up the defeat in his voice. "After the no-confidence vote, Bog was elected —"

"What about his personal droid?" Ferus asked. "The bribery evidence —"

"Vader shut down the HoloNet," Dinko said. "Didn't you know? And we've gotten word the comm system might go down. And the ministers . . . we tried . . . Bog claimed evidence was planted during the ten minutes his droid was missing during the assassination attempt —"

"That's ridiculous. It was in sight the whole time. I can testify to that —"

"It doesn't matter. Bog's first ruling was to outlaw all personal droids, and he gave his own up as a gesture of solidarity with the law. They are blaming the Roshans, saying that they can infiltrate our systems through our PDs —"

The comm system began to crackle. "Get them out," Dinko said.

"What about Larker?" Ferus asked, but the comm went silent.

"It's eerie," Flame said. "Look below."

Below, the people of Sath were lining up to turn in their personal droids. Collection sites had been set up quickly, operated by Imperial stormtroopers and officers.

"This is only the first step, I'm sure. They're giving up their freedom for nothing," Robbyn Sark said. "We can't hurt them."

Sadness filled the craft as they flew through Sath.

Ferus flew past the outskirts and hugged the ground, flying low and hoping to avoid detection. The Crystal Forest rose ahead of them. In the setting sun, it flashed bloodred. Flame keyed in the coordinates to her ship.

Ferus flew through the crystal canyons, squeezing through narrow openings and speeding past incredible formations. Soon he landed next to Flame's sleek red ship.

"I'm counting on you," Ferus told her.

"I'll deliver them safely," Flame said. "And then I'm sure we'll meet again. There's lots of work to do."

The group quickly climbed out of the speeder.

"Thank you," Robbyn Sark told Ferus.

"You have the information," Ferus said. "Use it if you can. When you get back to Rosha, I'll get you in touch with the resistance here. There's someone named Firefolk who can work with you."

Sark nodded. He turned and helped his fellow delegates board Flame's ship. She ran lightly up the ramp.

Trever turned to him. "Aren't you coming?"

"No."

"But there's nothing left for you to do here."

"I have to get Firefolk in touch with the Roshans when things settle down. And I can't just disappear. Vader will be expecting my report."

"But he told you to bring him the thief. He's looking for me. If you don't bring me to him —"

"He's bluffing. He can't hurt me. Not yet. The Emperor still wants me around. Trever, you have to go."

"Why are you staying?" Trever looked at him angrily. "I don't get it. This could be your only chance to leave, and you're staying!"

"Trever!" Flame called. "We've got to go now!"

"Go," Ferus said. "Promise me you'll get back to the base."

Trever held his gaze. He said nothing.

Trever turned his back and started up the ramp.

"No matter what, I'll find you!" Ferus called.

Trever didn't turn.

Ferus felt a wrenching in his heart, a feeling he was making a terrible mistake. He stood, watching the ship take off.

May the Force be with him.

CHAPTER EIGHTEEN

Ferus sensed the change in activity as he entered Imperial headquarters. Officers rushed by. Service droids were loaded onto gravsleds. Bog Divinian had been legally elected, and now the Imperials could truly take charge.

"Ferus!"

Aaren Larker appeared, coming out of a narrow side corridor. He beckoned to Ferus, who followed him into a small meeting room.

"I was hoping I would find you."

"I'm sorry about the vote."

"I should have seen it coming," Larker said bitterly. "I counted on the loyalty of those who once were my friends. And now my Roshan friend will die for my blindness."

"Robbyn Sark is safe, I hope," Ferus reported. "By now he should be off-planet and on his way to Rosha."

"Thank the stars," Larker said. "Now, I have a proposition for you. I heard that you've been ordered to find the thief of Bog's droid. No doubt Vader wants you to produce anyone with ties to Rosha."

"I can produce no one," Ferus said.

"Yes, you can," Larker said. "Me."

"You didn't steal Bog's droid," Ferus said.

"So you do know who stole it." Larker smiled. "Nonetheless, I will take the credit for it."

"I don't understand."

"Vader is going to turn this city upside down just to prove a point. I can't let that happen. I can give this to my city, at least."

"I won't let you do it," Ferus said. "You'll be arrested."

"They won't arrest me," Larker argued. "I may not be the prime minister any longer, but I still have enough of a following on Samaria for them to be cautious. I can claim that I was trying to find evidence of Bog's bribes. The accusation is out there, thanks to the resistance. There will be some who'll believe me. It's worth a shot if I'm to keep my base of support."

Larker put his hand on Ferus's arm. "I'm the only one Vader will believe. And if he has an excuse to go raiding the city, you and I know he'll use it as an excuse to locate any resistance members."

"Vader hardly needs an excuse."

"Sath doesn't need any more unrest. I promise

you, as long as I agree to publicly support Bog's story, he'll let me go. They've gotten exactly what they wanted."

"I can't let you do this," Ferus said.

"It's done," Larker said, and walked out the door.

Two days later, Ferus sat in the BRT computer room, his head in his hands. He had just heard the news.

Aaren Larker had been arrested and charged with theft and conspiracy. He was taken to a Samarian prison. On his first day there, he was killed by a guard. Official reason: He was trying to escape.

Ferus had no doubt that Darth Vader had given the order to have him killed. Larker had underestimated Vader's cruelty. Vader didn't care about how it would look. All he wanted was control. Now he had it.

Dinko had been arrested. Ferus had been unable to contact Nek or Firefolk.

He'd heard no news from Rosha. With the HoloNet down, there was no way to hear anything except through official Imperial reports, which he could not trust.

He still didn't know if the Roshan delegation had made it out of Samarian airspace, but he assumed Flame had been successful or he would have heard.

He felt a surge of sickness wash over him, and

he raised his head just in time to see Darth Vader at his door. Loathing and rage surged through him.

Murderer, he thought.

"The inauguration is starting soon."

Ferus stood.

"The HoloNet is back up again," Vader said. "Perhaps you will be interested in its first broadcast."

Vader waved his gloved hand over the sensor, and the screen blazed to life.

At first, Ferus couldn't make sense of what he was seeing. Explosions. Stormtroopers rushing through an official building. But it wasn't Sath he was looking at.

The Samarian announcer spoke in triumphant tones. "The invasion of Rosha has begun. Their constant refusals to allow Samarian access to their technologies has resulted in a blow for liberty."

Smoke and fire. Devastation and destruction.

And there, a landing platform with a sleek red ship now a smoking ruin. Blown apart.

"The members of the Roshan delegation that fled Samarian jurisdiction were among the first casualties. Bog Divinian's attempted assassination has been avenged. . . ."

The words faded against the roaring in Ferus's ears. Robbyn Sark's body, crumpled on the platform. Other bodies. Twisted metal. An outflung hand.

Trever . . .

"It's time to go," Vader said.

Ferus put one foot in front of the other. As he did, something shattered inside him. He had failed. He had miscalculated everything. The battalion had been on alert to invade Rosha, not Samaria. He had sent the delegation and Trever straight into the midst of the fighting.

He had failed them all.

Trever huddled under a blanket. Flame crouched near a fire, warming up a protein meal she'd scrounged from somewhere. There was no power in the capital city, and the Roshans were making do where they could. Fires had sprung up in empty lots around the city and in the parks. Those who had lost their homes in the bombings had gathered what possessions they could and set up camps. So far the Empire had looked the other way.

They both wore hoods, to disguise the fact that they weren't Roshans. Flame had cleaned her face of the smoke, and now a livid red burn marked her forehead.

He owed his life to her.

She'd dragged him from the burning transport, concealed him in a utility cart, and somehow gotten them both out of the landing platform and away from the blasterfire and the roar of the explosions. She'd made him keep walking when he didn't want to walk. She'd found cloaks for them that concealed their burned and blackened clothing.

Someone nearby in the park had a portable vidscreen. The HoloNet news was playing. Trever turned away. This was all too familiar. The invasion. The stormtroopers. The blasting of Imperial propaganda on all vidscreens.

He'd seen it all before on Bellassa. He couldn't bear it again. How could he bear it?

"And today, Bog Divinian took on his official duties as ruler of Samaria," a voice boomed. "At his side were the Ministers of State, as well as invited guests. The Emperor sent his congratulations."

Trever looked over. On the vidscreen he could see Bog, in a purple cape made of thick veda cloth. On one side stood Darth Vader. On the other, Ferus.

Trever froze.

"Still trust him?" Flame was standing, looking at the vidscreen, her hands gripping the tray of food.

Trever swallowed. "Sure."

She crouched down next to him. Her eyes were vivid green underneath the red burn. It would leave a scar.

"Bog is ruler. Aaren Larker is dead. Dinko was arrested. And here, on Rosha — they knew we were coming," she said. "They were waiting for us, Trever. It was an ambush. How did they know?"

His gaze moved from her pale face and blazing eyes back to the vidscreen.

Ferus walked through the cheering crowd. In lockstep with Darth Vader.

It was an ambush. How did they know?

Trever's eyes burned, and it wasn't from the smoke.

How did they know, Ferus?